First published in 2023
by Shay P. Leighton for
Tough Guy Book Club

www.toughguybookclub.com

Cover illustration by Cara Jane Diffey
Cover design by Chris Capetanakis
Typeset by Chris Capetanakis

ISBN: 9780645524826

CONTENTS

Introduction, by Shay P. Leighton
Founder and Chair of Tough Guy Book Club

What story would you tell?

In my life, I've spent a lot of time talking to people in pubs over a drink, and I've heard a lot of tall tales. Each of them as unique as the person telling them.

I've always been interested in the stories that make people.

The loud heroic one about the mighty fishing trip. The hilarious one about a huge night on the town. An earnest one about how they met their partner. A quiet one about their father. People are a collection of stories, it's what makes us.

So, what happens when you take a group of men from every walk of life from across Australia and tell them they have a month to deliver a short story? Well, we wanted to find out...

Welcome to **Short Stories By Goons—Volume 1**, the first in a collection of short stories written by members of the **Tough Guy Book Club**. This collection of short stories represents the amazing combination of culture, history and creativity that is the **Tough Guy Book Club**—a once tiny book club that all started with a couple of mates getting together to talk books over a beer.

Tough Guy Book Club is about stories, it's about reading books, hitting the pub, and having big, boisterous conversations about the kind of thing that people shy away from these days. For too long the pokie machine, the cover band, and the TV have left the men in our pubs to have boring conversations. Where has our storytelling gone? I don't want to sit in a pub and hear about the weather or some TV show. I want to sit in a pub and argue about the nature of revenge with some guys who have just finished the **The Count of Monte Cristo**.

Every month, we ask the Goons that attend **Tough Guy Book Club** to complete a challenge. These Monthly Challenges are sometimes a simple task that's good for your health, like checking your blood pressure. Sometimes they are weird, like guerrilla gardening—that's good for your community. Other times they are meant to push our Goons out of their comfort zone. This is the result of one of those challenges.

The history of the Australian pub is the history of people telling tall tales, and our club is firmly a part of that tradition. It's not much of a challenge for our Goons to tell a tall tale in a pub, trust me—it's usually harder to stop them. But what if we challenged the Goons to take it seriously? What if we challenged them to write the best story they could? Perhaps it would end up being one they would be proud to share with others, rather than to laugh it off.

Short Stories By Goon—Volume 1 features sixteen amazing short stories from across Australia (and one from the USA)—each one crafted by a member of our book club. But good pub stories need to come from some struggle so there was a catch... Each story had to mention two elements: a key and an offer. And they needed to be written in the month of October. We figured those constraints would be a solid starting point for some pretty damn good stories—and the Goons didn't disappoint.

Whether you like reading thrilling fantasy adventures, modern romance or thoughtful observations on life, this volume has something for you. So settle in with your favourite drink, and discover a new group of Australian writers.

I would like to thank our amazing, dedicated volunteers whose love and hard work keep this club running in its 80 current locations.

Without you, I would still be reading by myself in pubs and I probably wouldn't be here.

I would also like to thank our amazing celebrity judges, the Minister for Creative Industries, the Honourable Steve Dimopoulos MP, the wonderful Megan Washington, and artist Curran James.

Everyone has got a story, if you take the time to listen.

Cheers,

Shay P. Leighton.

THE JUDGES

The Victorian Minster for Creative Industries, a pop star, and a tattoo artist walk into a bar. They are there to judge a short story competition...

The Honourable Steve Dimopoulos, MP

Before entering Parliament, Steve ran a local café, worked with refugees and migrant communities in the courts, and worked for a federal politician. He also served as a councillor and Mayor of the City of Monash.

Steve believes that governments can help people create better lives for themselves. This is what prompted him to run for Parliament.

The priorities Steve has for his community are to help create excellent public institutions and services from schools to transport to health care. He believes that these services are vital to address the sharpest end of disadvantage and ensure that everyone has the best chance for a good life.

Steve's vision for Victoria's future is that it is a place in which businesses can be successful, where there is more economic activity, employment and wealth for his community. Steve says that governments have the power to create better public infrastructure, policy stability and incentives for business to grow and prosper.

The areas of public policy that he is most passionate about are justice, mental health, a sustainable environment and the economy.

He was appointed to the role of Minister for Creative Industries and Minister for Tourism, Sport and Major Events in June 2022.

Megan Washington

Megan Washington is an ARIA award winning singer and songwriter. Now working as a screenwriter and composer for the ABC, you can listen to her podcast CrossBread, which she co-created with Kate McLennan, Aaron Chen and Chris Ryan.

Curran James

Curran is a Darkinjung/Wonnarua tattoo artist and illustrator originally from Newcastle, NSW. Now living in Melbourne, he currently works at Crucible Tattoo Co. Kensington and is Shay's preferred tattoo artist.

You can see Curran's work on his Instagram account, @curranjamestattoo and on the Crucible Tattoo Co. website — www.crucibletattooco.com.au

SHORT STORIES BY GOONS

VOLUME I

A delightful short story with beguiling characters and a satisfying fool's errand twist.
Megan Washington.

I found it both facetious and playful, but layered with regret. Something heartfelt but unattainable. Or maybe it just made me smile when I needed it.
Curran James.

WHEN THE POST OFFICE CLOSES,
BY ALEXANDER DANCE
CHAPTER – YARRAVILLE, VIC

Probably no one really knows why the town of Opportunity got the name it did.

If it was named in earnest, then it was named a long time ago. Long before most residents in the town remember.

Most of those left remember, at least, when the mill was still running, largely because very few people have moved there since. Back then there was enough to make the community infrastructure viable. Not a thriving town, but perfectly viable.

When it closed abruptly one April, over 700 direct and indirect employees were suddenly without work and Opportunity began its downwards trend.

First the local football club disbanded. Then the local primary school due to diminished enrolment. When the top pub closed its doors, leaving only one drinking establishment left for 40km in any direction, even the most stubborn local began to feel the inevitable.

But they say when the General Post Office closes is the true point of no return for a country town.

This was an idea that Michael Lyons had put very little thought to, despite having recently stuck up a notice on the door of the Opportunity GPO that informed anyone who read it that all post for the Opportunity township will be run out of the Woulburn GPO.

Michael probably would not have been able to tell you the Woulburn GPO was a 47 kilometre drive.

What Michael was thinking about, as he stood opposite the locked post boxes inside the Opportunity Post Office, was what his regional manager had said to him earlier this week.

"I've got a very important assignment for you Lyons," he had announced across the office floor, "this is the kind of thing that could really get you noticed."

If Michael was the kind of person that noticed sideways glances and knowing smiles, he may have not been the only person in the office that day that took this statement for what it was. Instead he had a smile stretching ear to ear as the regional manager pulled him aside.

"Now Head Office want me to go out there and get this done," he continued, "But I've got a lot going on here, so I've got an offer for you: you head out there and get this done, make sure you get it all wrapped up, keep it under your hat, and I'll make sure it isn't forgotten."

People in the regional head office generally knew Michael was ambitious. But he suffered from a rather unfortunate form of this driving impulse. He was afflicted by both ambition and gullibility.

This resulted in the unfortunate combination of wanting to do the right things to get ahead, while also being completely and easily suggestible to exactly what those things might be. Because the problem with blindly buying into motivational corporate slogans like "hard work is always rewarded" and then following them unchecked, is certain people will usually find a way to make the hard work you're doing mostly consist of all the work they don't want to do.

And with Michael that is usually what they did.

So with hopes of establishing himself as the guy you go to in the Australian Post Regional head office when you want a job done right, Michael Lyons had arrived earlier that day in Opportunity's only scheduled bus run.

"I'm heading back in two hours," the driver had shouted as he disembarked. He was the only one who had booked a return ticket. Not just that day either. It had taken him quite some time to convince the lady at the ticket counter this was actually what he wanted. Opportunity did not get a lot of day-trippers.

In those two hours he needed to walk to the Post Office, tape his sign to the door, unlock and empty each of the 121 active locked post boxes, and get back to the bus stop.

Google Maps had told him the walk from the station to the post office was going to cost him seven minutes each way. So if he accounted for 10 minutes of incidental time that left him with 96 minutes to open, label, and clear 121 locked boxes. Or, more precisely, just over 47 seconds per box.

That was a rate Michael had determined he could maintain thanks to a dry-run he had performed at a local Post Office under the watch of that branch's bemused general manager.

It was, however, a plan that was predicated on all 121 active locked boxes having their corresponding keys hanging on a hook in the cupboard behind the counter. Which was the reality that was crashing down on Michael as he stood across from the wall of post office lock boxes.

Each one had its door hanging open and its key dangling in its place in the keyhole. Every one except one box.

Box 77.

The two silver number sevens shone across at him. The three flat head screws fixing each one to the locked door were positioned almost like two eyes and a round mouth, mocking him as he stood there unable to pull their door open, and check the inside of the post box, which was in all likelihood going to be completely empty.

Most of the other ones were, but Michael's regional manager was very clear. He needed to put up the notice, empty out every lock box of its existing post, and lock the doors. The boxes had to be empty before Australia Post could officially close the post office.

It wasn't that the box couldn't be opened eventually. Obviously they would be able to get clearance to break open the box eventually, Michael just wasn't authorised to open it by force. And that meant he wouldn't be able to officially finish the job. It would also mean paperwork for the regional manager.

Michael sighed and turned from the wall of boxes. Every drawer and cupboard in the post office was opened and rifled through. His return trip had long left the bus-stop. He would be staying at the Opportunity Hotel that night.

He took his time tidying up the result of his whirlwind search, and then made his way outside. There wasn't much else to do except to go book a room and then find a seat at the bar downstairs. Michael didn't really like beer but he knew from his many business social functions that struggling through a few pints was, at the very least, a way to pass some time.

He pushed out the door and turned to lock it. The bell on the frame of the door rang loudly and unevenly and something to his right moved. A man was sleeping against the wall on the Post Office veranda.

He rolled over and slurred, "Issit open?"

Michael turned the key in the lock, the man spoke with a thick accent which threw him off for a moment. "Uh. No," he finally said.

The man half sat up, and let out a cough with a sharp crack at the back of it, "Nev'r opens on time."

With some effort he brought his feet around in front of him and slowly worked his way to his feet. Michael was never very good with accent, and the effect the man's state was having on his voice wasn't helping but he thought maybe it was from somewhere in the UK.

"Well, um..."

The man looked at him waiting. Talking with people naturally was one of the key aspects Michael knew he needed to work on if he really wanted to advance professionally. He had read his fair share of self-help best sellers with the aim of finding a more natural temperament when it came to casual conversation, but when the moments came his mind tended to jam up with hesitation.

Right now he was the local representative for Australia Post, and though this man seemed not exactly in his clearest mind, it was really Michael's responsibility to explain to him exactly what it was he was doing.

A professional tone, or in fact any words at all, failed to come. Eventually he nodded and shrugged at the same time, and then pointed at the A4 piece of paper taped to the door.

If this gesture was confusing to the old man he didn't display any outwards signs of it. He moved past Michael and squinted to read the short message underneath the Australia Post letterhead.

He turned to Michael, "You did this?"

"Yes, that's right."

The man turned back to the sign, and rasped his fingernails across his cheeks in contemplation.

Michael was finally getting a more official line about the situation together when the man turned on his heel down to the road and began ambling off toward the Opportunity Hotel. Michael breathed the type of sigh that usually followed a survived social interaction and then followed him.

It took him about three times longer to make it to the Hotel than it otherwise might have been because Michael didn't want to walk past the old man, and he wasn't moving with much urgency. At one stage he stopped completely for a few minutes.

But they made it through the door eventually.

There were only two people in the Hotel when they entered, the bartender and a portly man sitting in the middle of the bar. But both pairs of eyes went straight to him and completely ignored the old man as he made a bee-line for a stool at the end of the bar and slumped there with no apparent attempt to get the bartender's attention.

Michael chose a stool on the other side of the portly man, two spaces down.

Without a word being said the thick set bartender started pouring a pint and then set it down in front of the old man, he then slowly walked the length of the bar towards Michael and greeted him with a stony glare.

Michael felt a sudden urge to clear his throat. Through a cough he managed, "Could I have a pint, please?"

The bartender's eyes flicked down to the logo on Michael's polo and back up again, "You're the bloke that's come to shut down the Post Office, then?"

"Well, umm..." Michael glanced at the beer taps but the bartender stood unmoving with his arms crossed across his broad chest, "not exactly."

"What do you mean, not exactly?"

"Well, Australia Post doesn't actually run regional post offices, they are franchised to local operators. When the last franchisee, Gilbert Henry, stepped down..."

"Gil had a heart attack."

Just when Michael thought he was getting a bit of rhythm, "Right, yes. Well in any case, when he could no longer run his franchise, we advertised for someone else to take it over. When there wasn't any interest we were forced to discontinue the franchise."

The bartender still hadn't moved, "How is that different to shutting us down?"

"Well, we won't, um, it's not exactly that we are shutting down the post office. We just haven't got anyone to run it."

"But it's not opening any more?"

"Uh, no," the bartender continued to stare him down, Michael reached for some more insight he could offer and found none, "Would I be able to get that pint?"

The bartender grunted and turned to the taps. He tilted a glass under the spout, flicked the handle down and waited as the white jet filled it up.

"So, are you finished?" he asked over his shoulder.

Michael assumed he was still talking to him but couldn't work out what he meant so he said nothing.

The handle of the tap flicked back up and the bartender watched while the frenzy of bubbles settled into a solid inch of foam. Then he looked up, "The post office. Have you officially shut us down?"

"Oh right. Well, technically no."

The bartender stood holding his pint. It seemed Michael was going to need to give him more if he wanted his drink.

"All the locked mailboxes have to be cleared out and the mail forwarded to the Woulburn. But I couldn't open all the boxes because there was a key missing."

Then, almost jokingly, he added, "You don't know who has box 77?"

He said this last bit as a vain attempt to garner a little bit of approval, and maybe even get the pint he ordered. The last thing he expected was an answer.

But the bartender placed the pint in front of him and said, "That'd be Charlie's."

Michael sat up a bit straighter, "Who's Charlie?"

"The bloke you followed in."

Michael looked at the end of the bar. The old man from the post office was barely managing to balance the glass to his lips.

"How did you know what number his box was?"

"I didn't know the number, but if it's the only one with the key missing, then it'd be Charlie."

"But why does he have the master copy?"

The bartender shrugged, he looked over at the man sleeping on the end of his bar, "He's waiting on a letter from his wife."

"A letter from his wife? I can let him in to open the box."

The portly man sitting two stools down from Michael let out a short bark of a laugh at this. Michael turned to him.

The man didn't look at him but smirked into his pint and said, "He's been waiting on that letter for 22 years."

The bartender looked with disapproval at this comment, but said nothing, so Michael decided to turn his focus to the new figure.

"What does that mean?"

The new man finished a long drink that finished his glass and raised a finger to the bartender, who began pouring another.

"Nothing mate," he said, "I just don't think there's much chance of you getting that key."

"But why not?" Michael moved across the two stools between them, "I really need that key."

The Portly man considered this, "That key is...important to him."

Michael shook his head, "But he still keeps his mail with the postal service. His mail will just get diverted to Woulburn."

"There's a little bit more to it than that."

The portly man turned to look at the old man who was now asleep on the bar with the nearly full pint in front of him, "Charlie's been around here a long time. He moved here from London when there was still a bit of promise in this town. Early 1980's. The mill was still up and going and there was a lot of momentum with mining all over Australia in remote communities like this."

"But it never really happened for Opportunity. As you might be able to guess."

He let out another bark. The bartender had supplied him a new pint, Michael remembered his own drink in front of him and screwed up his face as he took a tiny sip and continued to listen.

"But Charlie had put a lot of his eggs into it going the other way. If you asked him at the time, he reckoned he was getting information from somewhere."

"After a few years he brought his wife out too. They were newly-weds. He'd obviously painted a picture for her about what it was going to be like for them here. They were going to make their fortune."

Another sharp bark.

"It wasn't long before it was clear it wasn't going to happen. Old Charlie just dug in though, sunk more money in, God knows where it was coming from. His wife wasn't built for the hard life and she could see the money disappearing that could have been helping them live the life she wanted back in London."

The bartender interrupted, "Alright Hawks. That's enough, mate."

The man acknowledged this with a nod and pulled back a bit, "Anyway long story short. She left, and that finally broke Charlie-boy. He has no idea where she went, so he can't follow her. Can't even send her mail. So he just hangs around, checks his mailbox once a day, hoping today is the day a letter from her finally arrives."

The man looked over, meeting Michael's eyes for the first time, "All he's got really."

Michael looked past the man at the bar at Charlie, "That's... that's really horrible. I mean what a story."

The portly man granted this with a small nod.

Michael was letting all this sink in. Then he thought about that locked box down the road, and then about walking back into the regional office to tell the manager he couldn't get the job done. Even with his lack of social subtlety, he knew what he was going to say next was going to sound trivial, but he couldn't really think of any other way to say it.

"The thing is, I still really need to empty all of those lock boxes. And really, he isn't supposed to have the master key for the box, that is always supposed to stay at the GPO."

The portly man at the bar raised an eyebrow at this. Michael sighed.

"I really need to get that key."

"Well," said the man, turning on the stool and gesturing towards Charlie, "You can ask him. But I don't think he'll give it up."

"All his mail will still be directed to the Woulburn post office. It will all still get to him."

The man turned back facing the bar again, "Yeah, I know. I don't think that's really what it is about."

Michael nodded. He picked up his beer and winced as took down another sip, then he stood and walked down the bar to sit down next to where Charlie was sleeping.

He cleared his throat.

"Excuse me, sir."

He glanced back down the bar, both the bartender and the man were watching him.

He spoke again, a bit louder.

"Excuse me, Charlie?"

He put his hand on his shoulder and shook him gently. Charlie's head stirred, and then his bleary-eyed face rose up from the arm it was resting in. He blinked hard and then seemed to focus on Michael's face.

"We met down at the post office, remember?"

Charlie's face creased in concentration, weighing up the situation he had just been woken up to. Eventually he nodded.

"I'm from Australia Post," Michael pointed to the logo on his shirt.

Charlie's face uncreased slightly. He repeated his nod.

Michael looked back down the bar, both sets of eyes were still on him. He returned to Charlie.

"I... uh. I understand you're waiting on a letter from your... uh, your wife?"

This made Charlie's face stretch in an entirely different direction, one eyebrow shooting up and the opposite eye squinting down. Michael was unable to tell if he was more drunk than hungover but some combination of the two was clearly making it difficult for him to bring his faculties to bear on what Michael was saying.

He pushed on regardless, "Well, as you saw, the Opportunity Post Office's franchise has been discontinued," he heard a loud bark of cough behind him, so he added, "I've come to close it down. The only thing I have left to do is clear out your box. Box 77. Which I believe you have the master key for."

Charlie stretched out his mouth a few times and then swallowed what was in it with a bit of effort. He didn't seem to be tracking with the conversation any more than he had previously but, maybe thinking he had nodded too many times already, he cleared his throat and said, "Righto."

"Now I've just been talking with..." he gestured down the bar realising he didn't actually know the man's name. The bartender had called him 'Hawksy' but Michael was uncomfortable using nicknames even for close acquaintances, "... this gentleman, and I understand why you might not want to hand me the key."

Charlie's eyes narrowed again, "Genn'lmen?"

"That's right, he explained your... situation, I guess. But I have a proposition for you."

"Wassat?"

"Pardon me?"

"Wassa proper-thing?"

"Oh, like an offer."

Charlie nodded, still deep creases in his face but seemingly getting his footing somewhat, so Michael continued.

"Well, whether you end up giving me the key or not, I'll be leaving town, the post office will be locked and you won't be able to get in to reach the lock box anyway."

He felt awful as soon as he said it. Charlie cocked his head to one side but Michael rushed on.

"That's just my job, you understand. If it wasn't me it would be someone else. I'm leaving town tomorrow morning. But what I can do..."

Michael paused to take a deep breath. He was trying to read Charlie's face but it was barely moving.

"I can take you down to the post office now and let you check your box yourself. One last time."

Charlie opened his mouth, and Michael's chest clenched in anticipation. But then Charlie seemed to think better of it and closed it again.

Michael waited a few more seconds, "I thought," he said finally, "it could be, like, closure. Of a sorts. At least."

Charlie's creases had gotten deeper again. He mouthed the word 'closure' a few times.

Michael looked back down the bar. His audience of two were still watching and he wished they weren't. He felt terrible. And he was sure it wasn't going to work.

"Yeah, alrigh' then," said Charlie, his voice still hoarse.

Michael's head snapped back, "Alright?"

"Yeah, yeah, c'mon. Less go." He drained the remaining three-quarters of a pint with a practiced sustained gulp. He hopped off the bar stool and headed toward the door.

Michael tried to follow suit, bringing the glass to his lips but only managing to take a little over an inch from the top. She slammed it down on the table and scampered off just reaching the door as it slammed shut in Charlie's wake.

He instantly narrowed his eyes as the glare of the bright orange landscape crashed into his eyes. Charlie was already on his way, ambling towards the post office. Michael walked double-time to catch up with him, but pulled up short, not being able to bring himself to walk beside him.

He watched as his odd stilted gait bounced him down, up, and then forward with each step and wondered sadly how many times he marched this route, from the front door of the Opportunity Hotel to the post office to open his mailbox and find no letter inside.

Already he was dreading the moment that was to come.

And yet nothing he had promised Charlie was a lie. He wasn't going to be able to use his key after Michael left anyway. Another Auspost employee would end up in Opportunity. One with authorisation to open the box by force, and then even if there was a letter inside he would just redirect it to Woulburn.

Michael shook his head at the hope he was already starting to foster. There wasn't going to be a letter. It had been 22 years. He was just trying to make himself feel better.

Stewing in his thoughts, Michael had dropped back a bit. Charlie had made it to the post office and was quietly looking up at the sign on the shop front awning.

Michael drew level with him and looked up and some unexamined instinct made him read the sign out loud.

"Opportunity General Post Office."

As he was saying the words, the irony of the town's name hit him for the first time.

Michael looked at Charlie, "Shall we go in?"

Charlie looked like he hadn't heard him at first. Then he nodded very slowly.

Michael walked up the steps, pushing his hand deep in the pocket for the keys, he pulled them out and picked out the right key and slid it into the lock. He looked up at Charlie.

"Now, just to be clear I need you to leave the key behind when you're done. In the lock-box, that bit's important."

Charlie gave him another one of his measuring stares. It seemed to Michael he'd sobered up considerably in the walk down from the hotel. He reached into his own pocket and pulled out a key. Hey looked down at it and then threw it up to Michael who caught it clumsily against his chest.

"You open it."

Michael looked down at his palm. A distinctly shaped post office lock box key lay there attached to an official Australia Post master key ring with two white sevens etched into the plastic.

At first he didn't understand, but then as he looked up at Charlie, looked into that aged stare, he thought he did. If this was to be the last time that lock-box opened, he didn't want to be the one to do it. He didn't want to end it.

Michael nodded solemnly, then turned the key and walked in.

The lock-boxes were exactly as he had left them. Every single one yawning open, keys dangling out the side of the open doors. All except one box, two thirds of the way along on the right about halfway up. *Box 77.*

Breathing to steel himself, Michael strode off towards the boxes. It took him only six steps and he found himself right in front of the two silver sevens.

Michael put the key into the vertical slot and turned it sideways. Despite himself he looked back at Charlie. His creased eyes didn't move from the box. Twenty-two years of waiting come down to the single action of opening a four by five inch lock box door.

Michael realised he was holding his breath.

He turned back to the box and lifted the front panel open.

There sitting on the floor of the lock box was a thin brown envelope. Written on the face of it in black looping handwriting it said:

Charles Mason
Locked Box 77
Opportunity, NSW 2311

Michael's breath sharply drew in. A letter. There was actually a letter.

In a flash of movement he looked back at Charlie. Could he see it from where he was standing? Could this be the letter? From her?

Charlie had barely moved.

With a trembling hand Michael reached in and picked up the letter. He turned with an outstretched arm and walked towards Charlie.

Without a word Charlie took the letter from him, tore it open, and pulled the sheaf of paper out from inside it.

And he started to read it.

The suspense was too much for Michael. "Is it..." he started.

Charlie looked up.

"Is it from her?"

Charlie nodded. Michael felt another sharp gasp of air suck into his lungs and Charlie continued to read.

Michael waited again, for as long as he could, but eventually it got too much from him again.

"What does it say?"

Charlie looked up. At first it didn't seem like he wanted to tell Michael and he was sorry he'd asked. But then, much like he had in the Hotel when he first agreed to come over to the post office with Michael, he spoke without warning.

"It says, she's hadda good time in Sydney and she's back on Tuesd'y. Needs me to pick 'er up from Broken Hill at 6."

Michael opened his mouth. If it was to say something he never got there as his jaw just hung there.

Charlie looked up at him and nodded, "Cheers, mate." Then he turned and walked out the door.

Michael wasn't sure how long he stood in the Opportunity Post Office after Charlie left, but eventually he locked the front door again and walked back to the Opportunity Hotel. The high of finally doing the job he was sent to do was somewhat diminished by the high of finding Charlie's wife's letter.

He booked a night at the Hotel and spent most of the rest of the time in the bar and when he walked back in the portly man who had told him about Charlie was sitting right where he left him.

His name turned out to be Robert Hawkins. As Michael enthusiastically recounted everything that happened, he had to admit that the story wasn't quite getting the reaction he expected.

A smirk slowly grew across Robert's face, a few times breaking into stifled gasps. When Michael finished, he called the bartender over and made him tell it again.

As the bar filled up Robert pulled each local over to get a fresh retelling. The reactions varied from bellowing laughter and a strong clap on the back, to a disbelieving shake of the head, usually, it seemed, in Robert's direction.

In the end he just put it down to them all just being happy for Charlie.

If Michael was the kind of person that noticed sideways glances and knowing smiles, he might have had a better idea of what was actually going on. But if he was that kind of person he probably wouldn't have been in Opportunity in the first place. And even if he somehow was in Opportunity, he probably wouldn't be the kind of person that just believed stories he heard at bars from men he'd never met before

And if that were the case, Michael would have left the next morning on the first and only bus out of Opportunity, maybe a little bit wiser but, also maybe, a little less interesting.

He didn't get much appreciation for closing down the post office, just a few grumbled comments about taking a day to empty a post office in the sticks. But Michael didn't care, he felt he had already gotten his reward when he handed that brown envelope over into Charlie's hands.

And he kept ploughing on with his unique form of gullible ambition, which somehow seemed to work for him. Because if there was something to be said for believing everything you're told, it's this: you end up a lot less cynical and with some much better stories.

This is a great world that the author created and as some in my team commented "I want to read more". I hope that the author considers expanding on the theme and takes it to the next level.
Steve Dimopoulos MP

BARTHEN'S HUNGER, BY JOSH GOODMAN
CHAPTER – DUDLEY, NSW

Barthen joined the milling crowd passing through the east gate in Sildjin. Barthen hated cities. He hated the stench, the claustrophobic buildings, but mostly he hated the people. He had loathed cities his entire, unnaturally long life but he had no choice but to visit them on occasion. His need drove him there. He had the last of his green qorin tattooed into his right arm, on top of numerous previous tattoos which left his skin a mottled green and brown mess. The tattoos were utilitarian, not for aesthetics. While the green qorin prolonged his life and allowed unnatural healing, it left him with a constant hunger. An unfillable void inside. Part of his inner self had become locked away and qorin was the key to prising it open, even if just for a time. Sometimes he wondered whether yielding to the forever sleep would be preferable to the constant hunger, however the hunger would not allow him to yield. It was like something wholly separate from him. An unseen master.

Pushing past the throng, he took solace under the eaves of a book merchant's shop. He checked the pouch in his inner coat pocket. It contained three small black tipped blow darts. That should be fine, he thought and proceeded down the cobblestoned road to the dock precinct to spend some kihts on information and pick up a lead.

~

Ria sat on her haunches in the dim entrance to an alley on Dock Street in the Sildjin night, her face hidden in her hood. Across the road her brother Gan was feigning sleep on a tattered blanket as a laden merchant cart rolled between them.

This is it, she thought, pleased with herself. Only two guards, and both look like they haven't drawn their swords in years.

The merchant was carrying furs and bolts of silk destined for his ship and then the outlying islands, no doubt. After the wagon passed her line of sight with Gan she signalled with a flick of her left hand and a flutter of fingers.

Gan jumped up and briskly walked past the two guards who trailed the wagon and called to the merchant who was sitting on the rear wagon box, "Iron kiht to spare? Please, sir?"

"Away, rat!" the merchant spat dismissively, not giving Gan a second look.

Gan sauntered past the merchant and, in an instant, he had grabbed a small bolt of silk and was half way down the alley. He wasn't the fastest street rat in the dock precinct, but the two pudgy guards looked like they hadn't run a mile since their distant youth.

The stunned guards took a moment to react, possibly feeling the effects of their ale from earlier in the evening.

"Go!" the merchant bellowed at them. Their momentary stupor vanished and they disappeared down the alley a moment later after the boy.

Ria slowly rose and slipped her hood down as she approached the merchant, her knife already in hand. She clicked her tongue trying to moisten the green powder she had just placed under it. The merchant, who made the portly guards look undernourished, started to yell for aid but Ria lifted her blade towards his neck and made a hushing sound.

"Your guards have been led deep into the dock precinct by now and won't hear you. Oh, and the city guards don't tend to spend too much time in this part of the city. If you value an intact neck above your kihts please remove the silver chest from the box you are sitting on".

Ria and Gan had been watching this merchant all day. Ria had followed him while he delivered some of the wares from his ship this morning and observed his handsome payments. The silver chest in the wooden box contained all the kihts her and her brother would need for a new life away from Sildjin and the difficult memories tied to the place.

Ria sensed someone and turned around. At the end of the street stood a man in a black cloak with a broad hat. There was no reaction when Ria looked in his direction. He remained perfectly still, observing.

Turning back to the merchant, "The box now!" Ria ordered. She checked over her shoulder again to ensure the dark stranger hadn't moved.

The shaken merchant fumbled with the lock before Ria grabbed the brass key and with effort shoved him aside. The small silver chest lay inside.

"I'm back!" Gan puffed with a big grin on his face, obviously proud he had lost the guards somewhere in the dock precinct warrens.

Ria opened the chest. It contained a weighty leather bag which she promptly passed to Gan.

"Go. I'll see you soon at the place" she said, giving him a quick warm smile.

Ria looked over her shoulder again to the motionless figure who was still there, watching. Not a moment later, a red-faced guard appeared from down one of the alley entrances. When he saw Ria he drew his sword, breathing heavily.

Great, she thought You didn't quite lose them as effectively as we'd planned, Gan!

With blade up, the panting guard started to advance. She could hear movement behind her too. The other guard? The stranger? She didn't have to wonder long. With cold shock, she looked down as a sword protruded through her middle and was then withdrawn. She clutched her stomach and fell to the ground. The second guard loomed over her still body.

"You let the boy with my kihts get away! Find him!" shrieked the merchant, spittle flying from his mouth.

With the guards off after Gan once more, Ria sat up and jumped to her feet. The green powder under her tongue having dissolved away. With a quick cheeky smile and a wave to the merchant, she darted down one of the alleys to meet up with Gan.

She left a stunned merchant in her wake and an impassive stranger down the street on the corner.

~

Barthen perched precariously on the rooftop of a back-alley tailor's shop watching his quarry in the courtyard below. Although the rain pattered softly on his broad hat he didn't seem to notice. He was transfixed on his prize. He subconsciously scratched at his right wrist, the green, elaborate tattoo which barely extended beyond his shirt cuff was still in the chaffing phase. Each new tattoo annoyed him at first but the convenience of qorin sitting under your skin and available for use whenever needed was too advantageous.

Although not large, the city of Sildjin seemed to attract all the miscreants from the surrounding towns and villages like vermin to refuse. It provided more than enough opportunities for these sorts to pilfer purses and extort the vulnerable. However, Barthen was not a lawman. He was not there to impose justice upon these poor fools, his focus was his hunger, on her.

He cared little about the thievery which we had witnessed. He cared that the girl had been run through and then nonchalantly ran away as if she had never been harmed. Although the ability to use qorin was rare, a city of this size could always be counted on to produce some people with the gift. Or curse, depending on your viewpoint.

Wherever there was a market for qorin, there would be someone willing to meet the market with supply of the illicit, controlled substance. Wars have been fought over the stuff and wars have been won, or lost, because of qorin. The qorin guild's secret refinement process meant that it maintained a very high price, which governments reluctantly paid. It also meant that the small amount that made its way on the black market captured a hefty price. This girl is either earning good coin as a thief or has stolen some.

Barthen scratched at his tattoo again and the rain still softly fell around him.

Below, a spindly boy with an overcoat about three sizes too big passed the girl some flat bread and said, "I left them so far behind, Ri!"

Barthen could only just make out their speech over the soft rain.

"Well, maybe if you weren't so fast they would have followed you a bit further rather than coming back to stab me!" she replied with a raised eyebrow. "We got what we were after nonetheless. Tomorrow we'll buy some fancy clothes and pay our way on a caravan to Kabrahti to start over."

Gan shook his head vehemently. "Kabrahti? I thought we were going West? We want to go further from the capital, not towards it!"

"Don't worry, Kabrahti will be safe," Ria assured. "If we don't steal anymore, then I won't need to risk healing myself anymore! With the silver kihts we have after tonight, we'll have more than enough to rent a stall to sell lamotka pastries in the markets and make a living. We'll have a new life. Remember the pastries I used to bake with mama?"

Gan nodded solemnly.

"Things will be better there, Gan, I promise" she reassured him, placing her hand on his wet back.

The clouds had given all they had and the rain petered out.

Barthen slid his hand into his cloak's left inside pocket and carefully withdrew his blow dart tube and the small pouch of darts tipped with a black liquid. He loaded the long black pipe and put it to his mouth.

Ria's hand reflexively sprung to her neck, flicking the dart off her and into the night as she spun around.

Barthen jumped off the roof with his midnight black cloak billowing behind him. His legs gave a barely audible crack when he landed but he paid no mind to the fractures. His fresh tattoo tingled slightly as he advanced towards the surprised Ria.

"Run, Gan!" she ordered while staring at Barthen, "I'll deal with our friend." She slipped a knife out of the small of her back and held it towards the approaching dark figure. Gan ran towards a rear alley but hid behind some stacked apple crates. Terror written on his small grimy face.

"Stay back" Ria warned, slicing the air in front of Barthen. The edges of his mouth turned up slightly as he brandished his own knife from his belt.

Beginning to circle his quarry, Barthen asked, "You have qorin, you have the gift and evidently know how to use it. You're out of your depth, girl. Lead me to your supplier and you may see out the night?"

Ria had never been bested and had never faced another qorin user. One side of Ria's mouth raised in reply. She began to circle the gaunt, black-clad man and he circled too.

"Do you know what black qorin is, girl?" Barthen said is his slow deliberate way. He noted the flash of confusion on her face and smiled.

"Well, you're about to find out. I suggest you take me up on my offer. All I want is to know where you get your qorin."

"I think I'll take my chances with you, old man. I'd have no chance of living out the day if I gave you what you wanted."

As if in some kind of dark dancing ritual, both Ria and Barthen lunged forward and planted their blades deep within the other. Now in an embrace, Barthen's smile extended as he whispered into Ria's ear, "This power was never meant for you, young one," and with that he stepped back. The warm trickle of blood from his side subsiding as he felt his fresh green tattoo prickle again.

Ria fell to her knees, her face awash with shock. Gan screamed, "Ria!" and rushed to her as she collapsed completely, her eyes glazing over.

"Heal, Ria!" Gan pleaded, sobbing.

Barthen pushed the hysterical boy to the ground and pulled a small glass container of emerald green powder out of Ria's jacket. He pocketed the substance, grabbed the boy by the collar and brought him close.

"There is no need for you to join your sister in the forever sleep tonight. Who supplied her qorin?" Barthen's low and measured voice almost whispered to the boy.

Gan hesitated and without meeting Barthen's eyes whimpered a response.

Barthen stood and walked out of the courtyard, scratching his right forearm as he left behind him a boy weeping over his sister.

Barthen's hunger led him on.

One of the rules of Tough Guy Book Club is that we don't talk about work. But this story is a beautiful reflection on the nature of work in our post-industrial age, while meditatively contemplating the downfall of our colleagues.
Daniel Carlin, Director of Tough Guy Book Club.

THE BUTLER, BY D. R. LEONARD
CHAPTER – WILLIAMSTOWN, VIC

I

Tick, tock.

The sun rises, casting shafts of light over the ridge and into the valley floor.

The stately home, unchanged in centuries, illuminates in the morning glow. The light reflects from windows and banks of solar arrays, bouncing off the surface of ornamental ponds, bringing colour to the blooming hedgerows and freshly mown lawns.

Inside the house the butler starts his day. He throws back the heavy drapes allowing daylight to spill through, picking out the details in the room, penetrating dark corners.

First, he clears the plates. The food remains untouched. He disposes of the waste, washes the plates, and returns them to the kitchen. Moving through the large silent rooms he cleans as he goes, ensuring no items are out of place and there is no build-up of dirt or dust to spoil the fading grandeur. The house is so much quieter now, and the stillness makes his job easier.

Finally arriving at the front-door he reaches into his pocket and removes the key given to him on his first day in the job. It is old, heavy, and mechanical, calling back a time when information still arrived in physical form. Unlocking and opening the door, swinging it wide on well-oiled hinges, the butler steps out into the day. He begins cutting, weeding, clearing. He keeps the gardens at showcase perfection, all the way to the boundary wire where his responsibility ends.

Beyond the fences and hedgerows nature has taken over. Trees grow rugged and wild, bereft of shape and pruning, and moss and brambles have long since choked out the paths and roads which once connected the house to the wider world. This is not the butler's concern, and he keeps his attention on maintaining this small oasis of order within the chaos of his surroundings.

2

It hadn't always been like this. Once there had been gardeners, cooks, maids; a small army of help to share in the maintenance and keep the household machinery running smoothly, all the while pandering to the needs and whims of the masters of the house.

He had come here voluntarily to lead this army, to direct and control and participate. The Lord of the Manor, an obscenely wealthy and paranoid man, had wanted to ensure his loyalty and had made him an offer he could not refuse.

Taking him out of the grinding poverty, soaring crime, and intensifying pollution of the vast, faltering urban sprawl the majority of humanity lived in, he was provided with a rare opportunity to live in the increasingly remote world of the elites. Here comfort and luxury were commonplace and even the lowest workers were able to enjoy a safe and healthy lifestyle that was not possible to find elsewhere.

He was offered unlimited food, housing, medical-care, and security in exchange for a lifetime of commitment to the family and their home. And it only cost him his free will.

3

The operation itself was quick and painless. Developments in neurobiology had reached the point where the decision-making areas of the brain had been mapped, explored, analysed, understood. A small chunk of grey matter was removed, replaced with a microscopic collection of chips and wires which caused his thinking to be... different.

It wasn't that he could no longer think for himself, but the neural pathways and reward circuits were delicately re-wired to pull his thoughts in the direction of how he could best serve the household and its masters, how best to maintain the grounds and meet their needs, and how to constantly improve and do better.

He threw himself into his new role with gusto, enjoying the peace of mind that comes with having all material needs met; of being warm, comfortable, safe, and well fed, without fear of the future or concern of imminent danger.

At first his new way of thinking caused no anxiety or conflict. He wanted to succeed and please his new employers. He enjoyed his new-found power and responsibility. The house ran like clockwork with the butler guiding and directing proceedings and only occasionally getting his hands dirty. He was the model employee, busy without being frantic, well-mannered without being obsequious, but over time the edges began to fray.

A part of his consciousness became disengaged from his stream of thoughts and sat apart from them, watching his actions but unable to influence the outcome. A prisoner in his own mind he became an observer, aware of what his body was doing but unable to break into its stream of politeness and activity. To outward appearances he remained the perfect chief of staff, deferring to his employers and efficiently directing his subordinates, but inside his frustration grew at his inability to engage in even the slightest act of rebellion, never uttering a cross or disrespectful word, never indulging his appetites beyond that which was necessary to keep himself fit and functioning.

As the years passed a further obsession emerged. Should he spot any piece of work which had been incorrectly completed by another staff member, an item out of place, an unweeded garden bed or an unwashed item of cutlery, a need to correct it grew within him to the point where it became physically painful. He either needed to resolve the issue himself or take the offending staff member to task with such vigour that they vowed never to let it happen again.

So far as his masters were concerned everything was going as expected. As the outside world sank further into decay, thanks to the butler's work the manor house remained a glistening tribute to what had once been possible and a window into a way of life from earlier times, up until the accident.

4

They had been cutting back the birch trees lining the driveway, a thankless and repetitive task which never seemed to be fully completed.

The butler was currently fixated with the cleanliness of the line created by the trees when viewed from the front gate and was personally supervising that afternoon's activity. The difficulty of precisely trimming the branches, combined with the need for a specific vantage point to assess the results, lead to a growing frustration within the butler that the outcome was not meeting his very particular standards.

After the third or fourth unsatisfactory attempt to create the perfect line the butler loudly claimed that he would do the job himself, grabbed the pruning saw from the struggling groundskeeper and marched toward the offending branch.

He was not used to manual labour and wielded the saw with far more enthusiasm than competence. Having climbed a ladder to gain access to the branch, he balanced himself in such a way that he could grip the saw with both hands and set to work.

Shortly after he had started the saw-blade caught and jammed itself in the branch mid stroke, catching the butler off balance. He toppled from his perch and fell awkwardly to the ground; his unexpected motion causing the ladder to sway and then topple. The initial impact shattered one of his legs, and the subsequent crash of the ladder ended in a visceral crunch as his other leg was also broken.

The groundsman rushed to his aid, but by then it was too late.

5

As the wider world became a more dangerous and inhospitable place, the owners of the house had resolved to make themselves self-sufficient. They used the opportunities provided by their wealth to remove the need to venture outside.

To this end the house was equipped with state-of-the-art medical facilities, and it was within these that the robotic surgeons assessed the results of the accident and realised the futility of attempting to repair what remained of his legs. His employers were true to their word and spared no expense to aid his recovery. Two prosthetic limbs were fashioned, metal and plastic replacing flesh and bone, and electronic motors replacing the need for muscle and sinew. A connection through his spine provided full control over his new legs. During his rehabilitation he found that not only was he able to walk again but, in many ways, his performance was superior to his unaugmented state.

He was able to walk the estate for hours at a time without tiring, checking and re-checking the state of the house and grounds and moving with a swiftness unfamiliar to his previous self. This increased efficiency did not remain un-noticed by his modified reasoning, and soon he was consumed by thoughts on how he could further improve his capabilities.

More accidents followed, continuing the fateful trajectory started on the day of the pruning saw mishap. In a succession of engineered tragedies, his hands were caught in lawnmower blades, his arms shattered by falling masonry, his eyes blinded by a misplaced pitchfork, his hearing destroyed by a pierced eardrum. After each accident there followed a short stay at the infirmary, during which a new technological marvel was fashioned and installed. Each one making him slightly more effective, and slightly less human.

Throughout all this his disengaged consciousness watched on in horror, appalled at his actions but unable to stop them, not realising that there was worse to come.

6

Now aware of his shortcomings in the practicalities of maintaining the estate, he studied the roles and activities of the other staff members, watching and practicing should the occasion arise once more where he needed to step in. Over time he became fully conversant in all the jobs required to keep the house running properly: from the maintenance of the grounds and the organisation and cleanliness of the rooms, through to how the family liked their meals to be prepared, and when they liked to receive them. He became competent in gardening, landscaping, cookery, and laundry. He developed a craftsman's eye for any construction or repairs needed to prevent the house from falling into decay or disrepair.

His improved physical capabilities meant that not only could he complete all these tasks as well as the other staff members, but he could in fact perform them better. This realisation ran around and around in his mind. If he could get better results than anyone else, should he take over the completion of everything?

As this rationale settled as fact, he watched as he was drawn to the inevitable conclusion.

7

The accidents resumed, although this time it was not the butler who suffered. One by one the other staff members met their untimely demise through a range of unlikely circumstances. The car slipped off its jack while the mechanic was underneath. The caretaker fell from the roof while repairing the tiles. The cook died from exposure, having been trapped in the freezer overnight. Each of the accidents explainable but invariably fatal, and each time the butler stepped in and continued their work with no disruption.

As the number of household staff dwindled, the remaining few grimly realised the shape of events. But with no proof, there was little that could be done. The only person with whom they could raise their concerns was the butler, as only he had the ear of their employer. However, those who spoke to him only hastened their own departure.

Towards the end their thoughts turned towards escape, but there was no longer anywhere to go to, nor any way to get there. Before long he was the only one left.

The masters of the house either didn't notice or didn't concern themselves with the details, so long as everything was done to their satisfaction. They were getting old themselves now and, in watching the decay of the world beyond their fences, had decided not to create a new generation. They lived out their lives in the comfort of the luxury they had built, with the service of their loyal and resourceful butler.

8

The years passed and the demands of the residents fell away. The aging butler continued to replace each of his failing parts with the fabrications from the medical bay. There was no longer any need for the accidents as his body was wearing out naturally. His remaining muscles, bones and internal organs were slowly but surely replaced by mechanical substitutes, each finely manufactured to ensure his continued operation.

Eventually only the brain remained, preserved in a bath of electrolytes. His remaining spark of humanity watching remotely, as if from a great height.

The masters were now mere husks. Centuries old and bed-ridden, kept alive through machinery and feeding tubes, unable to move or think. He still cooks for them, just in case, and clears away the plates each morning.

The house and grounds are kept immaculate.

The door is locked with the old key in the evening and unlocked again each morning to start afresh.

The butler completes his work and retires for the night.

Tick, tock.

The sun rises.

The butler starts his day.

And inside, behind his eyes, he is screaming.

Daniel McMahon knows too much about the inner workings of our book club. Another Daniel with this much information is dangerous and he must be stopped... But the story is pretty good.
Daniel Carlin, Director of Tough Guy Book Club.

BOOK CLUB NIGHT, BY DANIEL MCMAHON
CHAPTER – PENRITH, NSW

It's book club night.

Every third Thursday of the month is book club night. Dunno why they picked the third Thursday. It's one of a number of arbitrary rules in my book club. Rule one, first name basis. Rule two, you don't have to finish the book, and you're not supposed to spoil the ending for people who haven't. Which seems a bit fucken silly, joining a book club with no intention of reading the book, but anyway. Rule three, be tolerant and respectful and fucken blah blah blah... you get it.

Speaking of arbitrary, turns out Liv forgot I was going to book club tonight. Even though it's the same Thursday it always is. Even though she's the one who told me to join a book club if I wanted to get out of the house more. Things have been tough lately and we need to talk, she says. Well, that's her fucken problem, isn't it?

Slam goes the front door behind me and she can say it all she fucken wants. I'm already walking.

An arbitrary rule of my book club which I actually like is that it takes place in the lounge of the Lord Edgbaston, which is my local pub.

I cross the street past the servo and there it is - three stories of dark red brick with lights glimmering gold in the upstairs windows.

Inside it's even better. Wood panelled walls and manky carpet. Empty except for a bunch of regulars at one end of the bar, a pile of newspapers at the other, twice as old and just as full of shit.

I love the Edgy. Even Liv loves the Edgy, though we haven't been here together in years. That would defeat the purpose, wouldn't it? I stroll up and order my beer and sink the first three inches before the lady even gives back my card. Standing there, eyes closed and lost in delicious cold foamy thoughts, I wonder if I need to go to book club at all. This is my meditation.

I'm gonna go, of course. I came this far. Through the back past the toilets to the staircase. Halfway up there's a turn beneath a big portrait of dead Lord Edgy himself. I never pay much attention to it but this time it starts talking to me.

"There he is! Jay, my good fellow. An inestimable pleasure as always."

Jesus. It's not the portrait talking, obviously, it's this bloke on the stairs. Tartan trousers, blazer with leather elbows, old brogues - the whole getup. Jay's my name, if you were wondering. I dunno what this guy's name is and I don't fucken care. I just call him the Professor.

"Hey... mate."

"You come armed with reading material and refreshment, I see!" he nods at the book in one of my hands, beer in the other, "Pardon me while I procure some myself."

And he flounces past me down the stairs. What a fucken performance, right? Chucking around all those extra words just to show everyone he knows them. Gives me the shits. If you want to know how much I like the Edgy and book club just remember that I put up with the fucken Professor once a month.

Up onto the landing, down the hall to the lounge and...

"Heeeyyy! Hello again! Welcome! Right on time!"

There they all are. The ones that know me, even the ones that don't mumbling along to be friendly. There's Patrick Bateman, Fat Goth Chick, Matron and Mister Woke and Silent Steve. Patrick Bateman always turns up in a suit, Fat Goth Chick is pretty self-explanatory. Matron is an older lady, Mister Woke says shit like 'problematic' and 'decolonisation', Silent Steve isn't named Steve but I call him that because he sits in a corner, sips his red wine, never says a fucken word.

Tonight there's also Indian Dude who's been a couple of times and Asian Girl and two others who I've never seen before. And that's my book club. Fucken diverse bunch, aren't we?

"Lovely to have you back, Jay. Grab a seat."

Oh, and there's Anthea.

Anthea is the president of the book club, or the 'moderator' as she says because nobody is supposed to be in charge. She's young and hot but smart too, with her vintage dresses and rockabilly tattoos and endless patience. I haven't told Liv who runs the book club, put it that way.

"Thanks," I say, and do as she says.

The lounge of the Edgy is a long dark room with a tiny bar that's never staffed on Thursdays, or maybe ever. All the mismatched armchairs have been dragged into a circle and there's an empty one next to Indian Dude, a sort of curly thing with blue satin cushions that he's waving at like crazy. I go over and sit in it, which seems to make him happy.

"Rishi," he says, "It's my third meeting but I'm still so nervous! Book club is such a new experience for me."

Not sure what he wants me to say to that but Anthea comes to the rescue.

"Okay, everyone!" she trills, "We'll get started. This month we've been reading..."

Speaking of diversity, one more thing. Another arbitrary rule of my book club is that we like to be inclusive and choose books by under-represented voices, especially women and authors of colour. This month's book is The Colour of Shade by Abeba Zuri Kikelomo. Bet you can guess how I feel about that one.

Well, you'd be fucken wrong.

I've read Shade twice. Read it last year when Kikelomo won the Storrier Prize and again for this. I think it's a brilliant meditation on political independence and an exquisite portrait of strained family loyalties. Since then I've read everything she's ever written. I think Kikelomo is the most important writer to come out of Africa since Achebe, a transcendentalist in the vein of Thoreau but with a tender human sensibility to match Rushdie or Garcia Marquez.

Yeah, you like that? The Professor's not the only smart cunt who can throw around fucken multi-syllables. Just because I don't do it all the time doesn't mean I haven't read every book there is. I just prefer to talk like a regular person and say what I fucken mean.

"Ruby, would you like to start?"

Ruby? Ah, Fat Goth Chick.

"Thanks, Thea. Um... I enjoyed it! It was pretty difficult - I usually read fantasy and horror, I think I mentioned that—so I only got about half way through but the parts I read were..."

And we're away.

Now before you assume I'm that piece of shit at the book club who talks over everybody, doesn't listen, and thinks he's right about everything, I'm absolutely not. Not the first two anyway. I am fucken right, at least around these people, but I'm happy to sit quietly and drink my beer and let them be fucken wrong before I offer my contribution. It's called democracy. While Fat Goth Chick is going through the greatest hits with Patrick Bateman and Mister Woke, I'm smiling and nodding like a good boy.

You want to know what kind of effort that takes, listen to this shit.

"Definitely took a while to get going. There were so many characters and names..."

"... and they're complex names. I don't want to say they all sound the same because that would be problematic. We just lack the frame of reference, you know..."

"I thought it was beautifully written though."

"Oh for sure. Like that bit at the start with the herd of buffalo..."

"That bit was so weird! I didn't understand, like, Imani says there's a famine?"

"They weren't real, right? That was the passing of her father's spirit from the end... that time travel element felt a bit like cultural appropriation to me..."

"... the father dies? Awww, spoilers!"

Everyone laughs and I wish I was deader than Imani's dad.

Look, I don't hate these people. I don't even think they're stupid or anything - Matron's pretty clever, even Patrick Bateman sometimes comes out with half-decent shit by accident. But nothing they say is going to change the truth about this book, or any other book, or the opinion I have locked up here in my skull. It's just fact. Do people have a problem with facts?

"Jay, you're very quiet. What did you think?"

Anthea's smiling at me. When things get bad she can always count on me to say something intelligent. A woman who wants to hear my opinion. Who would have thunk it, eh Liv?

"I think Kikelomo is the most significant —"

"Pardon me, so sorry everyone, would you mind terribly if I..."

It's the Professor. Sidling back into the lounge, carrying a big curvy glass of some beer that probably cost twenty fucken dollars and tastes like a fucken blueberry.

"Not a problem, Richard," says Anthea, "Jay, you were saying?"

The Professor sits in the last leather wing-back and crosses his legs at me. Before I would have sounded all spontaneous but now my rhythm's off.

"I think Kikelomo is the most important writer to come out of Africa since Achebe, a transcendentalist in the vein of Thoreau but with a tender human sensibility to match Rushdie or Garcia Marquez."

Everyone frowns, then nods, then goes 'Mmm' then stares in their lap and squirms a bit because they can't think of anything else to say. This is the reception my stuff usually gets.

I'm sucking down the last of my beer in celebration when the Professor says, "Fascinating."

What's fucken fascinating, Richard?

"What's fascinating, Richard?" says Anthea.

"Well, Jay and I are almost always on the same page, literally speaking. But I'm afraid in this instance, my friend... I couldn't disagree with you more."

His thoughtful silence is longer than mine. Except Fat Goth Chick and Matron and Indian Dude are all looking at him like they want to hear more. I lower my beer, not so much staring daggers as trying to stab the cunt with my chin.

"I think this is a disappointing work of genre fiction by a once-promising writer. I agree Kikelomo showed potential with her early work—Whispering Birds and The Waterhole in particular—but with Shade I think her politics have become muddy, her characters thin, her plots incoherent. I'm shocked that this won the Storrier..."

And away we go. Around the circle for another helping of under-baked fucken observations. The Professor looks at whoever's talking—elbow on knee, one hand cupping his chin like he's listening extra hard—but I don't for a second take my eyes off the fucken Professor.

Indian Dude first, "Actually, Richard—sorry, was it Richard?—Richard, I'm glad to hear you had some doubts too because I found the characters very unbelievable."

"Actually... yeah, now you mention it, the characters..."

"The character of Diallo in particular. I didn't understand why he would betray the village..."

"Which one was Diallo again? The cousin?"

"The uncle. For example, why would he ally himself with Colonel Gordon, especially after he ordered the soldiers to burn the house..."

"... for me they were all just very unlikeable characters. Like, I hated them all."

"But Diallo was possessed by an evil spirit, right? Imani says the ancestors are returning to the village, and some of them 'carry the sins of the past'..."

"... ohhh, okay. Yeah, that would explain a lot!"

And everyone laughs. Like missing the entire point of a book you've just read is fucken funny.

"You make an excellent point, Samantha, though for me the characters were not so much 'unlikeable' as 'transparent'. For me the underlying metaphor of the spirit world as a repository for colonialist trauma was, I'm sorry to say, painfully obvious..."

"No it wasn't."

If there were still some chuckles they're quiet now. The Professor, finally, is looking straight at me.

"I'm so sorry, Jay," he smiles, "I talked over you. Go on?"

"It's not obvious. It's woven subtly into the fabric of the novel. For example, Keilani's store in chapter nine has three floors, which is a clear allusion to the Inferno, Purgatorio and Paradiso of Dante's Divine Comedy..."

"Mm, I caught that reference too."

"... while in chapter sixteen Colonel Gordon builds the new church on the north side of the river, while Imani tends the livestock on the south side in a clear inversion of Animist and traditional Judeo-Christian theologies..."

Can't believe I said that but fuck it, big guns now. The Professor just squeezes his chin and his eyebrows and nods the whole way through my sentence.

"Very perceptive, Jay, I hadn't considered that. May I ask you an unrelated question? I'll ask the whole group in fact... has anyone here read Martin Thiong'o?"

This fucken guy. Polite little head-shakes all around. Patrick Bateman asks for the name again, takes out his phone, copies it down.

"N-G-apostrophe-O... have you, Jay?"

Now, whatever you think of me, I'm not the sort of guy who pretends to know something he doesn't. Not even in fights with Liv. So I have heard of Martin Thiong'o, I just haven't read him. May as well admit that because it's the truth.

Still feels like coughing up a big fat fucken turd when I say, "No."

Then I mumble in my lap, because if I look at the Professor any longer I'll fucken glass him, "Kikelomo is the most significant writer to come out of Africa since Achebe."

"Hah, agree to disagree, I suppose! But you should really try Thiong'o, Jay, you'd love him. A little earlier and more obscure, but his novel Darkness She Come was an enormous influence on my own writi... iiiiiinnnngggg..."

Well, that was fucken weird. I look up.

The Professor is still staring at me, but that's about all he's doing. The smile doesn't move and the moustache doesn't twitch and the eyes behind the chunky glasses don't blink. I look around the circle and the rest of them are frozen too - Patrick Bateman with thumbs on phone, Indian Dude furiously agreeing with Mister Woke, Silent Steve tipping a solid mass of red wine into his face.

I've done it. I've finally done it. I've broken the fucken book club.

"Congratulations, Jay."

I jump clear out of my chair. Behind me there's a voice, familiar but not, all echoey and shit like I'm hearing it in my chest instead of my ears. I turn around and there's Anthea, blonde hair floating even though there's no wind, green eyes actually glowing.

"S-sorry?"

"We have been watching you, Jay. For some time now. We thought perhaps Richard, but no. It is time for us to make ourselves known to you. You, Jay... are right."

I look around the circle for help but they're even less help than usual.

"About, um... about what?"

"So many things," says Anthea, "But in this case, The Colour Of Shade by Abeba Zuri Kikelomo. We have decided to grant you admission to the club within the club. The elite group where only the most exceptional books are read, the most complex opinions heard."

I knew it. I look over at the Professor, nudge his chair with my foot. He wobbles like a fucken cardboard cut-out.

"Nice," I say.

"You may enter," says Anthea, and she points.

The lounge bar of the Edgy might be tiny and unstaffed but there's a door behind it that wasn't there before. Low, set right in beneath the dusty shelf of booze. I go over and give it a shove but it's locked tight.

"How do I..."

"Take the glass, Jay. The beer tap is the key."

Christ I love the Edgy. Sure enough when I turn around there's a lovely chilled glass waiting on the counter. When I pull the beer tap the pipes groan a bit, but glorious liquid gold comes splashing out at the same time the door behind me groans open.

A staircase leads down into dark.

"Good luck, Jay."

I shoot Anthea one last look over my shoulder. This book club wasn't so bad, really. Least it got me out of the house.

I say, "Cheers!" and down I go.

Down black stone steps, past actual flaming torches in brackets on the walls. Looks like a fucken secret passage from something Fat Goth Chick would read. Some of the steps are wet and slimy and I have to be careful, take frequent breaks for refreshment. Feels like a long time before I see a faint glow at the bottom, which grows and grows until it becomes an arch.

The room I step into looks a lot like the lounge at the Edgy. Bit bigger, wood a bit darker, carpet a bit mankier. The armchairs are taller, with big carved arms, and there's a roaring stone fireplace that comes off as more creepy than cosy.

Twelve people staring at me out of hooded crimson robes doesn't help.

"Welcome, Jay..." says a voice in there, somewhere, "To the Circle of the Right. Be seated and we will begin."

One of the robes—I'll call him Fancy Robe because his has gold bits - sweeps a hand at the last armchair in the circle. I take a fortifying sip of my beer and do as I'm told. The chair might look a bit evil but it's fucken comfy.

"Jay," says Fancy Robe, "As the newest member of the Circle, you choose the book for discussion this evening."

I blink at him, "You don't set one every month?"

There's a weird snuffling noise around the circle. Takes me a second to figure out that all the robes are laughing.

"We do not require others to choose what we read," says Fancy, "You may select any book you wish. Your most esteemed authors and titles."

"How will I know you've all read it?"

"We have read everything."

Fancy Robe chucks his arms out and the last word booms around the walls like a cannon. I don't necessarily believe him but I like his style. Let's see what they've got.

"Have you read Don Quixote?"

"Yes."

"How about Solzhenitsyn's Gulag Archipelago?"

"Yes."

"A La Recherche Du Temps Perdu?"

I don't get the pronunciation right but fuck it. Go big or go home.

"Cover to cover, Jay."

Jesus, these Circle jerks aren't messing around. I only read Proust because Liv's parents came to stay and it was a slightly better way to pass the time than clamping my dick in the sandwich press.

"Alright. I'll go with one of my favourites. John Caden Caradoc's Midnight Dancer."

"An excellent choice. We shall begin!"

Fancy Robe's voice booms again and the fireplace whooshes up like dragon's breath.

"The book is J.C. Caradoc's 1951 masterpiece of detective-noir-slash-psychological-horror, Midnight Dancer. Opinions will be heard... now. Jay, would you like another beer?"

I look down at my glass, which I didn't even notice was empty, and nod back at Fancy. He does a wizardy hand-wave and someone else in a robe passes me a fresh one.

I think I might cry. I could fucken get used to this.

On the far side of the circle, a lady I'll call Scary Lesbian pushes her hood back, makes a tent out of her fingers and looks around at us all.

"John Caden Caradoc is the first author to truly capture the violence of the postwar American psyche."

Well, she's fucken right about that. Everyone does the snuffling noise again but this time it's lower pitched, more satisfied, like they're agreeing. Without any response or prompting a robe on the other side — we'll call him Eyebrows - shoves back his hood and joins in.

"The character of Adriana brilliantly subverts the femme fatale archetype while prefiguring the feminist writings of Shirley Jackson and Toni Morrison."

Fucken spot on, Eyebrows. I join in with the self-satisfied snuffling this time, wash it down with a righteous gulp of beer. Something hard in my stomach that's been there since I fought with Liv - and probably a lot fucken longer, honestly - unclenches a bit.

Next up is Kate. Dunno if she's called Kate but Kate's a nice name and I'm feeling generous.

"Detective McGillicuddy is a clear Christ figure, his three-day stakeout and eventual death at the hands of the gangster Danilowicz mirror the Passion Narrative."

Snuffle-snuffle all around. Not me this time. My righteous gulp of beer spits up a bit. I cough and splutter and manage to choke out...

"No it's not."

Kate looks like my throat tastes. Scary Lesbian and Eyebrows and a bunch of other empty hoods are all staring at me. Fancy booms again.

"Jay, do not..."

"But she's wrong. Detective McGillicuddy isn't a Christ figure."

"The... theme of redemption is prevalent," Kate blinks at me, at Fancy, at me again, "When compared to the Gospel of Matthew..."

"It's got nothing to do with the fucken Gospel of Matthew!" the thing in my stomach has clenched again, "It's based on real-life LAPD homicide cases from the 1940s. JC Caradoc was a journalist, a committed atheist, and he disavowed religious allegories in his work until the day he fucken died!"

I'm on my feet, breathing hard. Kate and the others are looking at me like a fucken crazy person. I'm guessing this isn't an ordinary Thursday for this book club.

"Nevertheless, some critics mainta... aaaaiinnnnnnn..."

And wouldn't you know it, while I'm watching her Kate's whole body strobes and slows down and fucken freezes just like the Professor did.

"You've gotta be fucken kidding me," I say.

"Congratulations, Jay..."

There's Fancy, right on cue. He's pushed back his hood to reveal a fifty-something bloke with grey hair and designer stubble and an earring. His eyes are glowing and his voice has gone echoey like Anthea's but otherwise he looks exactly like Liv's fucken hairdresser.

"... we have been watching. We grant you admission to..."

"Yeah yeah," I wave him off, "I got that part upstairs. What the fuck's going on here? I thought this was the Circle of the Right."

Fancy smiles. I swear you can see the smug radiating off him with his magic powers.

"There is right, Jay, and then there is right. You, like us, seek purity of knowledge. Whether a book or a film or socio-political situation, you know there is always a better... a more correct opinion."

I mean, he's not wrong, but it doesn't make me feel any better.

"Fine. What do I do now?"

Fancy booms, "Behold!" and waves his hand, the fireplace roars for a second until the flames are sucked down to nothing with a puff of blue smoke. The whole stone hearth rotates slowly in the wall and there's an empty space behind it. A staircase, leading down.

I let out a big sigh. Just a couple of steps in that direction make me feel very tired, for some reason. Must be the big empty glass in my hand.

I hold it up, "Can I at least get another beer first?"

So I keep being right and I keep going down. From the Circle of the Right to the Ring of Correctitude, to the Nexus of Accuracy to the Brotherhood of the Immaculate Opinion. They're all pretty much the same - groups of ten or twelve people in big medieval rooms, with increasingly spooky furniture and wacky costumes. One of them had a pool table but I don't get to play. Another I'm pretty sure has a big screen TV but it's hidden behind a fucken tapestry. Oh, and the Brotherhood is all dudes, obviously. They wear hats.

And of course they're all fucken wrong. In the Hall of Unambiguity with a big fucken stuffed bear looming over me, some Filipino kid says Flavius Maximus technically invented science fiction. This ginger lady in the Fellowship Without Fault tries to tell me the priest in Barclay's The Taking of St Tropez is a symbol for Communism, which is pretty fucken wild. Some of them are wrong in fun ways, I'll grant you, like it takes a second to deconstruct exactly why they're wrong. But wrong's still fucken wrong any way you slice it.

Also they keep bringing me beers, via more and more magical methods, so by the time I get to the bottom I'm not exactly firing on all cylinders.

Comes a point where I'm alone in an empty room.

It's a very small room, not much bigger than a toilet cubicle. Which is unfortunate since by now I'm busting for a piss. I step off the last step into a narrow space, one electric light-bulb hanging from the ceiling. I'm thinking about sneaky slash in the corner but when I look down there's familiar manky carpet under my feet. In front of me is a door, which I don't often see closed, so I push it.

And I stumble back out onto the curb in front of the Edgy.

Warm night air whips the sweat off my forehead. I do a bit of a stagger, turn and look back up at the red brick fortress that is the Lord Edgbaston. The lights are all off now. The only illumination is the fluorescent glow from the servo across the street. Very slowly I turn left and right, looking for Fancy or Anthea or even the fucken Professor, even though I know they're not there.

It's like I fell asleep in the loo and dreamed the whole fucken thing. Which would be a possibility except I seem to have retained an absolute skinful.

The Edgy's my local, I told you that. Walking distance from home, even staggering distance, but this is verging on fucken crawling distance. I weave and stumble, have a close encounter with a wheelie bin. At one point I remember how badly I need to piss because there's a hot trickle down my leg, and I yank myself out just in time to direct most of it into a flower bed.

Finally I reach the door I slammed, however many hours ago. I take out my key, stick my tongue between my teeth and try to perform some brain surgery on the lock.

Believe it or not I manage to get it open in complete silence, slip into the house undetected. I'm down the hall and halfway to fucken freedom when I hear a breath, turn and see Liv stretched out on the living room couch. Legs hooked over the arm, not even looking at me.

She's reading a book because of course she is.

"Sorry I'm so late. Everyone enjoyed the book so much we lost track of time."

That's what I plan to say anyway. What comes out is mostly consonants, with a hiccup in the middle that tastes a bit like spew. Liv calmly folds down a page corner—use a bookmark, for Christ's sake—and looks up at me.

"What are we doing here, Jay?" she says.

Now that's a complicated question. I'm not sure I have the correct answer so I play it safe and go back to the facts. Bit more effort on the diction this time.

"You're the one who said I should join a book club, now I'm not allowed to go?"

"I asked if you could skip one meeting so we could talk. You went anyway and now you're back at four in the morning stinking drunk."

"I've had a tough evening, thank you. Anthea—she's the moderator —well, her voice went all echoey and I went down a secret passage and had magical beers because I'm the chosen one..."

Liv laughs. Through her nose though, the very-not funny kind.

"Jesus, Jay. You're a lot of things but you've never been a liar."

"It's the fucken truth!"

I say it too loud. Way too loud. And I know I'm right but for once it doesn't seem to fucken matter. Liv flinches and I go stiff, and before either of us can do anything there's little footsteps over our heads.

"Daddy?" says a voice from the stairs.

Liv shoves me aside like a bouncer, stands in the doorway so I'm not visible.

"Daddy's okay, Jessie, he's coming up to bed in a second, okay?"

"Um, okay."

Little footsteps back the other way.

Liv turns to me and for a second I think her face has frozen. Like maybe some cunt in a robe is going to turn up and spin my bookshelf around to reveal a staircase that leads down to another house, another family. But it's just Liv. Her blue eyes might be glowing or it might just be years of fucken hurt and resentment shining like candle-flames in the little tear-drops.

"We're done," she says, holding one palm up in my face, "That's what I wanted to tell you—I have the papers ready. Had them ready for a while. You sign them, we'll share Jessie. Joint custody, she can go where she wants, whatever is best for her. You fight me, I'll kick you out of this house and you'll never see her again. So what's it gonna be?"

I sway a bit. Maybe the booze, or what she just said. It's a tricky one because she's probably right. It would be better for Jessie, for everyone really. We can be civil and tolerant and respectful about this, like our own little two-person book club.

"One time offer, Jay. Take it or leave it."

Then again, I've spent the whole evening being right and where the fuck did it get me?

"Leave the fucken papers," I say, "I'll read them in the morning."

SOLITAIRE, BY FRANK LIESS
CHAPTER – PORTLAND, OREGON, USA

Terry,

I'm guessing that the last thing you ever expected was to open your mailbox and find a letter from Charles Willington. After all, we haven't laid eyes on each other for fifteen years, or at least you haven't laid eyes on me. Sorry, old friend, that certainly sounds creepy as fuck; I suppose this entire missive is going to sound creepy as fuck, so I might as well get right to it: *I'm writing this from the future.*

I know what you're thinking, but I can assure you that I haven't lost my mind. No, I didn't spend the last fifteen years in the looney bin. I've been living a relatively normal, uneventful life in Portland, Oregon with my mother and a beagle named Charlie. They're dead now. Natural causes for both. Early last year. You might have seen my mom's obit in the Star newspaper. She still had a lot of friends in Ventura, or at least many folks who would remember her, which is why I sent the Star her obituary. I wrote it myself and I tried to present her life in the best light possible. I think she would have been pleased. I just figured many people in our former hometown would be interested in hearing about her demise, and a few would probably be relieved. What was I going to tell you about? Oh, yes, THE FUTURE!

It all started with a game of solitaire. Mom and Charlie had both passed away within days of each other. Charlie was heartbroken by her death and simply lost his will to live. He was really her dog, even though I was the one who brought him home from the shelter. They had an instant bond the moment they met. I was disappointed by the betrayal, of course, but seeing how devoted they were to each other was truly inspirational. It really was. Charlie was glued to her hip.

They would sit up at night and watch TV together—Mom stuffing Charlie with peanut butter pretzels, even though he was terribly overweight—and I would distract myself from contemplating my sad, lonely life by playing video games and the occasional game of solitaire. I always enjoyed playing solitaire with a real deck of cards. There's just something more satisfying about the old school tactile experience than playing on a screen.

During this particular round of solitaire, something unusual happened. It was a relatively small thing, but unusual, nonetheless. I was about to put a red jack on a black queen. I mean, I was simply thinking about the move and the next thing I knew, it had already happened. Did I black out for a moment? Grief can cause a lot of stress and stress can cause all kinds of ailments. You may recall that my mom was most concerned about my ailments, whether real or invented by her for attention from medical professionals. In any case, I decided I must have blacked out or was simply confused, but then it happened again. I was thinking about putting a black three on a red four and instantly the move had already been made! What did it mean? It was like I was suddenly transported a second or two into the future! Please don't throw this letter away! Hear me out and I promise you that you will be convinced that I inadvertently discovered the secret of Time Travel!

Over the next several months, I completely immersed myself in games of solitaire. I took a leave of absence from my job at the insurance company so I could play hundreds of games a day! I was a man obsessed. I rarely changed out of my pyjamas or showered. I had food delivered by Uber. I grew a full beard and looked like a crazed Rip Van Winkle. But it was worth it, or so I believed.

Over time, the future moves increased. I was absolutely ecstatic the first time TWO moves happened at once! Up until that day, I still wasn't entirely sure whether it was reality or just my imagination stoked by some kind of bizarre mental affliction. After that, everything accelerated. THREE moves at once! FOUR moves at once! FIVE! SIX! TEN! It finally reached a point where an entire game was completed immediately after I shuffled the deck of cards! I determined that the fastest time I ever completed a normal game of solitaire was about five minutes. Five minutes into the future! Oddly, my watch never indicated that lapse in time. I began to suspect that the time travel was only temporary. Once I moved forward in time, I was immediately propelled back into the present—springing forward and then snapping right back like a rubber band. However, moving forward in time DID result in permanent changes! The game of solitaire remained completed in PRESENT TIME!

I'm certainly not a physicist. I simply don't have the IQ necessary to get my head wrapped around what was happening. I did some research on the Internet about Space Time, Quantum Physics, Relativity. I wish I had the scientific ability to understand it. Perhaps things wouldn't have gone so terribly, horribly wrong!

I decided to try to move forward in time without playing a game of solitaire. Looking back, I'm truly ashamed of my folly. My hubris brought me into a realm that should not be entered by any man! But I'm getting ahead of myself. I'll try to explain what happened, step by step. I unfurled one of Mom's yoga mats and sat like a Brahman in the middle of the living room floor. Mom had a large hourglass that she used for decorative purposes, but it was completely functional. I placed the hourglass on the coffee table in front of me, turned it over and closed my eyes. I only had my eyes shut for a second. When I opened them, I was disappointed to see that the sand in the hourglass was draining just as one would expect. However, the house was filled with the smell of a fresh-baked pie. The frozen pie I had placed in the oven a mere five minutes earlier was completely baked! The baking time should have been at least an hour!

I duplicated this trick dozens of times over the next two weeks without any issues. Every item I placed in the oven was finished baking almost instantly. Pies, TV dinners, potatoes. It worked better than a microwave! However, upon return from one of my time traveling sojourns, I discovered something quite strange and rather shocking. I opened my eyes and discovered that not only was the 20-pound turkey in the oven completely cooked, but every figurine in my mother's curio cabinet had also been smashed to bits! Every one of them! You may remember that my mom collected those Tiny Forest Folk figurines-- little mice dressed like cobblers and such. She had hundreds of them and somehow, they were all destroyed within the estimated four hours I was absent! Who or what did it? I had no clue. They weren't just broken, they were pulverised, and the hammer used for the wreckage was displayed on the coffee table as though someone had deliberately left it there for me to find. I should have taken that destruction as a warning, but I didn't. Instead, I continued the escalation of my time travel experiments, and this is where my story takes the most gruesome turn. I apologise for bringing you into this, but I really have no other choice.

I never considered that my corporeal form actually went into the future when I initiated these episodes, but I am convinced that is exactly what happens. I am transported into the future and an empty space is left behind in the present. I believe the Universe is most particular about such anomalies. It won't just allow empty spaces in Existence. Those spaces must be filled, even if it is filled by Dark Matter from another dimension. I believe that is how The One Who Fills the Gaps was created. Again, I'm probably getting way ahead in the tale for you to follow, and I once again apologise. I'll go back to when the nightmare began.

I was putting on quite a lot of weight, what with all the baking of pies and turkeys. I decided to try my experiment by literally waiting for paint to dry. I painted my living room a lovely shade of periwinkle blue. I estimated that it would take at least four hours to completely dry. I took up my position on the yoga mat, turned over the hourglass and closed my eyes. When I opened my eyes, I was confronted with the most horrific scene imaginable. The periwinkle blue was contrasted by bloody red gore splattered from floor to ceiling. On the floor next to me was the mutilated corpse of my housekeeper, Mrs. Locke! She had been butchered! Almost completely decapitated! I almost fainted. Honestly, Terry, I don't know how I stayed conscious. I opened my mouth to scream but was suddenly struck mute by what I saw on the wall in front of me. Written in bloody letters: WELCOME HOME, CHARLES!

I didn't know what to do. It instantly occurred to me that I would be held responsible for Mrs. Locke's murder. It happened in my house and from what I surmised was committed using one of the knives from my own kitchen. I decided that even though I was completely innocent (now, I'm not so sure that is even true), I had to cover up the crime. I rolled Mrs. Locke's body into a tarp and dragged it into the basement.

After burying poor Mrs. Locke, I vowed to never attempt time travel again. I even went so far as to burn every deck of cards in the house, just in case I ever felt some kind of irresistible urge to engage in that profane activity again. This is where I'll admit to only you, Terry, that being able to move forward and backward in time comes with a certain feeling of ultimate power that can seem almost...godlike. I've never used drugs like you did when we were in high school, but I can imagine that the addictive qualities of time travel and your devotion to cannabis are similar. I hope I didn't just offend you with that comparison. I just don't know how else to describe it.

The police came to my door only once looking for Mrs. Locke. One of her neighbour's reported her missing, but she didn't have any close family or concerned relatives to spur on a large scale or sustained search. I simply told the officers that I knew very little about her and when she did not arrive for her weekly cleaning chores and didn't answer my phone calls, I assumed she had discontinued our employment arrangement and was doing something else. Frankly, the police seemed largely uninterested in finding Mrs. Locke. They were oafish and thoroughly incompetent, in my opinion. No one ever asked to search the house. Thank God! My sloppy cement masonry on the basement floor would have been a dead give-away!

Of course, my nightmare didn't end there, Terry. You know me, life has just brought me down one sad path of disaster to another! While I never intended to time travel again, The One Who Fills the Gaps had other ideas–sinister, EVIL ideas! One evening, I fell asleep on the sofa while watching that 1970's TV movie The Night Strangler with Darrin McGavin. It's one of my favourites and I've seen it dozens of times. Well. it's ruined for me now! Imagine my horror when I awoke to find the most gruesome scene from that movie recreated in my own dining room!

Four corpses had been propped up in the chairs surrounding the dining table. They had all been dispatched in the same way; with their throats slit from ear to ear. It appeared that they had been dressed in fine clothing post-mortem–I recognised my best suit and mother's favourite Easter dress among the costumes. A complete holiday dinner had been prepared and set up before the lifeless party. Mother's best china, silver and fanciest linens were appropriately and thoughtfully displayed before full serving trays of turkey, ham and all the fixings. It honestly must have taken all day to prepare. I had to bite my hand to stop myself from screaming out loud. I actually drew blood and have a circular scar from the tooth marks.

It took me quite a long time to compose myself. I genuinely considered suicide, but I've never been mentally strong enough to achieve that ultimate finality. Eventually, I set about the task of cleaning up the mess and disposing of the bodies. I dug two more graves and buried two of the victims in each one. No one ever came looking for those poor people. I scanned the news for any information about them. Sadly, there were never any missing persons reports about anyone that matched their descriptions. I surmised that The One Who Fills the Gaps chose the members of his grisly dinner party very carefully. Perhaps they were homeless and hungry, and he promised them a sumptuous meal–a meal that went untouched by anything other than mother's china and the garbage disposal!

The One Who Fills the Gaps was quite a successful and prolific serial killer, Terry, I lost count of the number of clean-up operations that were left to me. I had no control over when, where and for how long my time travel sojourns would take place. I was utterly helpless and my unknown, unseen nemesis seemed to take delight in torturing me more than anything else. In addition to fulfilling his insatiable blood-lust, his murderous rampages were clearly intended to fill me with shock and disgust. I won't even give you the details of what I call 'The Beagle Rescue Incident,' as I know you and I share the same love of animals, particularly dogs. It was truly horrible, Terry! HORRIBLE! I know it may sound odd, considering the incredible loss of human life, but it was the immeasurable cruelty that he inflicted on those innocents that steeled my resolve to do whatever I could to stop him.

I had to practice in small increments. Somehow, I knew that any sustained time travel episodes would summon The One Who Fills the Gaps. Nevertheless, after several weeks, I could actually feel the power growing within me. It's impossible to explain to anyone who doesn't possess this particular ability. I'll just say that it felt like there was a battery inside my body that was swelling with POWER. Finally, I just knew that the time was right. I closed my eyes, and when I opened them again, I was a full TWO YEARS in the future! I also knew that I was out of reach of The One Who Fills the Gaps. Oh, but he had been busy!

I found myself in a dilapidated cabin in Southwest Oregon. Scattered throughout the rustic decor, I found myriad newspaper clippings memorialising the heinous escapades of The One Who Fills the Gaps for the past 24 months. My house had been searched shortly after my disappearance and no fewer than 15 bodies had been found buried in the basement or unceremoniously stuffed into crawl spaces. They were calling the killer the Portland Strangler. I thought they could have come up with a more inventive name, what with all of the various methods of murder and mayhem witnessed by that house. Nevertheless, law enforcement had a dragnet out for me. The news reports stated that I was either the prime suspect or a potential victim of a killer or killers who should be considered armed and extremely dangerous.

I had also been very busy these past two years, Terry, for among the newspaper clippings I found a dirty gym bag that contained no less than two million dollars! Somehow, I had developed the ability to see briefly into the future long enough to scan sports scores and stock prices. By placing bets and investing my meagre 401(k) funds according to my foolproof prestidigitation, I had amassed quite a fortune. Of course, there wasn't much I could do to enjoy those funds, seeing how I was most probably headed for Oregon's death row at the Salem Penitentiary.

This is when I got the idea to involve you in all of this, Terry. I was able to make a trip back to your present time. It is a full month BEFORE my time traveling folly began. Right now, I'm probably sitting in my little house in Portland, enjoying a normal game of solitaire. I was able to mail the letter you are reading and complete a few other errands. I then travelled back into the future for the last time. I believe I am safe from any physical threat and I should be able to live out the rest of my days in quiet solitude, however, there is one thing I need you to help me with.

Inside the envelope this letter arrived in, you will find a small key. It is the key to a padlock. That padlock is affixed to the door of my old high school locker. You remember that locker, don't you, Terry? K-1408. It was right next to your locker. That's how we met and became such great friends. Inside that locker, you will find the dirty gym bag

I mentioned previously. Inside the gym bag, you will find the two million dollars. I'm offering that money to you, Terry, in exchange for your assistance with a very small task. The directions for that task are also in the bag. Terry, if you do this for me, you will be a rich man and every horrible act caused by my meddling with time will be reversed! Please do this, Terry! I assure you that many, many more innocent people will die if you do not!

> *Terry.*
> *If you are reading this note, it means that you were kind enough to open this locker and complete the task I requested of you. THANK YOU! As you can see, the money is all there. Two million dollars. It's all yours! I have to now apologise because the task is not without a high level of danger. I pray that it all goes to plan and that you do not get hurt in any way.*
>
> *Read this very carefully, Terry, and do exactly as instructed! At the bottom of the gym bag, you will find a pistol. It is a .357 magnum and it is already loaded and cocked. By the time you reach the end of this paragraph, The One Who Fills the Gaps will be directly behind you. He will kill you, if you do not kill him first. Get that gun in your hand, Terry! NOW! TURN AND FIRE!*

"So, who's the stiff, Fred?"

"A weirdo named Charles Willington. An insurance guy out of Portland. Looks like he made up some kind of crazy story to get his old high school buddy to kill him. Suicide by buddy."

"Wild, Fred, that's just wild. Well, his old friend put that hollow point slug right through his eyeball. I guess his plan worked. How did he get the guy to pop him?"

"All kinds of crazy stuff about time travel and such. It looks like the poor shooter is in shock. He had a bag full of cash, too, looks like about two million dollars."

"No shit?"

"Yup, sure glad I won't be dealing with this investigation. They have the FBI rolling in. Those guys can handle it, they have all the time in the world."

THE BALLAD OF RUDY WHITMAN, BY IAIN H. MCLEAN
CHAPTER – MELBOURNE CITY, VIC

Los Angeles, 2007.

I called it my black period. Painters have periods where they use nothing but red or focus only on blues and call it their azure period or some such. Not that I've ever really cared much for who painted what but if you don't appreciate art, there's not much left for you in this world. I'm not a complete heathen. In high school I asked my Modern Literature teacher if everyone was destined to have a mid-life crisis. Her response was I needn't worry, I probably wouldn't live that long. Well kiss my ass, Miss Park, here I am, still kicking around at forty-six. When it all goes down and the big kahuna destroys the world, the only thing I'll have to worry about is have I been true to myself? Look, I'm fat. I have hairy man-tits and I smoke. I was never built to last but that hasn't stopped me yet. So many people I knew had fallen from hard times to desperation, losing jobs, having cars repossessed, walking away from mortgages, declaring bankruptcy. In the scheme of things, I was lucky. I always had the green coming in. I always had enough to cover my tab at The Ranch. The Ranch was a hangout for guys who would rather be in a bar with a group of half-baked degenerates than at home with their woman, and at that point in time I had a woman. I had Erica. What Erica saw in me I'll never know. But my black period, man, that was something else. It pretty much started and ended with Erica. I call it my black period because most of the time we got blackout drunk and things were dark.

Erica was what other women would call elfin. Her natural blonde hair dyed red, more wood than blood, you get the picture, and her skin was that flawless type that very few people have. She stayed inside her whole life and still looked like she lived on Venice Beach. She had a killer figure and an infectious laugh. She oozed smut. If cancer was having a stag party, she'd be the stripper who'd ride him bareback just for laughs. She was dangerously addictive. Like I said, it was my black period.

Things worked well with us for a short time, then she quit her job as a hairdresser, told the world to fuck itself and reinvented herself overnight as a DJ. Hats off to her, within a fortnight she had a regular spot in San Pedro but that got old quickly and she moved to a bar in downtown Long Beach. It worked pretty well because back then my life involved mainly hanging round bars and restaurants at night getting photos of famous fuckups making a mess of themselves at parties. We'd hook up in the early hours after I'd clocked off. I'd go to the club she was playing and wait. In my business you know people. I know most of the doormen in town, and the dealers, so it was never hard to get in and score for free. I'd buy an old fashioned at the bar or if the waiter looked like some spotty school kid I'd just buy a plain old whiskey-soda. I hate explaining what an old fashioned is. Then I'd load up right there on the bar before making my way to Erica. We were living like rock stars until it started that each time we met she was more fucked up than me. I mean, that takes a serious commitment to chemical self-harm. When her moods changed more frequently than her panties I got to thinking: 'How is this being true to myself?' I like a buzz now and then, but I can live without it. She had chased the dragon so hard she'd caught up to it and nailed that motherfucker to the wall.

The game changer came in a bar called The Bullet. She was in the DJ booth when I got there. I got my whiskey soda and cut through the crowd. I was exhausted from sitting in my car all day so I didn't load up. She was surrounded by guys and girls as she slammed her body back and forth, waving one arm in the air in time with the music. She looked up at me as I approached. I waved. She smiled and beckoned me up. When I got to the booth my guts clenched tight. Some ripped big black dude was pumping her from behind. The crowd wasn't dancing, they were baying for more. Her denim shorts were on the floor, still hooked around her right ankle and their combined sweat ran down her thighs in rivulets. Then the asshole high-fived me like I was his basketball buddy. Fucking moron. He wore the whiskey and I force-fed him my glass. It was a jerk reaction. The blood exploded and he hit the deck. I left the place before anyone knew what had happened.

Next morning Erica was at my apartment. I don't know whether she wanted to make-up or not. She didn't get the chance. I had collected all of her belongings in a trash bag and left it outside my door with a post-it attached. The message was simple: 'classy'. I was out on assignment for most of the day working in Century City. When I got home that evening the bag was gone and a reciprocal message was on my door in what appeared to be lip gloss. It said 'YOU NEED HELP!' The fact she cared made me smile. I opened the door and my post-it fluttered down. It had been wedged in the jamb. On the back she'd written 'Adult Children of Alcoholics Anonymous. Glendale. Go there. Get help.'

I cracked the seal on a twelve-year-old single malt and settled down on the sofa for the evening. That was my life. Scotch and sofa. It was an okay way to relax between work. I had a feeling in my gut that I should be doing something more proactive with my time, like learning something or expanding my horizons but sometimes a sofa is too inviting. Most days after work given the option of a sofa or a slut, the sofa would win out.

As time rolled on we grew closer. My sofa and I started sharing whole days together, We got a larger television and upgraded to surround sound. DVD's were rented from the machine in the store on the corner or bought in bulk from guys peddling them in the Fashion District on the weekends.

When I felt the need to work, I couldn't. The jobs weren't paying what they had a few weeks before. It had been happening for a long time but I had turned a blind eye, telling myself it would somehow return to the levels it used to. Don't get me wrong, no photog has ever been a gazillionaire from selling snaps of some bint's cunt gum when she steps out of a town car on Sunset but we used to make a living. This is the only gig I've had. When I left school I wanted to be Ansel Adams. I worked every angle to get a job. I apprenticed under the best in the business. I've had shots in some major East Coast rags. But the money's in the dirt. I've spent every night of my adult life outside restaurants and hell-holes all over this city. It's all I know and now kids with laptops were killing the game. They were everywhere like flies. Pretty soon every network was in on the act, feeding of the kids that would do it for free. How was a guy in his mid-forties supposed to support his lifestyle? I spent most of my time in a car with a lens pointing out the window waiting for some schmuck to get out of a limo looking like they were hammered or trying to catch a game show hostess having an affair with a married actor. The business of being a paparazzo was not like it used to be, when guys shot film and hustled for real money. One website I tried to hock photos to offered me an 'image credit for my portfolio'. The guy cut the call when I asked how I could pay my rent by using a 'habitat services credit'.

Anyway, Erica was the only good thing I had going and looking back, I never had her. She had me. Then she dropped me. And I missed her chaos. She made the earth spin around the sun.

I'd had the post-it Erica stuck on my door in my billfold for months. I'd written on it the time and place of a meeting of adult children of alcoholics. Glendale was a bit of a trek. I mean, that's probably the reason I hadn't gone. My drinking was just about under control. It got out of hand for a while but I was back on top of it now. It's a cycle. My old man drank so it's ingrained in me to drink. Most people don't break the cycle. Most people don't go to AA meetings. They go to the liquor store instead. They're gutless wonders.

The meeting was in a church hall. Like that doesn't make you feel even more like a degenerate. The only people who have meetings in church halls have something to hide. Just sitting in the parking lot felt like I was being judged. Probably because there was a kindergarten next to the hall and it was early. Yummy mummies were picking up little girls and boys on their way home from the office. I looked like a sex pest lurking in his car.

A half-hour later two people arrived on foot. The middle-aged guy unlocked the door to the hall. He was accompanied by a woman in her thirties. Then a young man strode in. Then an old woman who seemed to be in her seventies. Mixed bag. I had figured everyone would be in their twenties, all pissing and moaning how they had been hard done by. There'd be the token earth mother and a fat fuck as well. No fatties turned up. One woman looked like she might have a friend who was a hippie but that was about it. They were mostly regular people. But they weren't. They were fucked up like me.

I went inside twenty minutes after the first couple arrived. A couple of wrong turns in the corridors and I got to the main hall. They had arranged three tables into a group and were sat around the perimeter. I took a seat slightly back from the rest. They all greeted me in their own way, one guy by openly saying, 'hi' but mostly through subtle gestures. The woman sitting next to me introduced herself as Marcy. She was the best of a sorry crew. After a couple of hours of over-sharing and prayers I got up to leave. Marcy patted my hand. She followed me with her eyes as I left the room.

Outside I combed my hair with my fingers then tried to assimilate the preceding two hours. What a headfuck. Most of them needed spine transplants. One or two were obviously working through issues and Jeff was beyond help. The alco-yellow-eye was a dead give-away.

Then Marcy appeared beside me.

"It takes some time to get into it, but you'll feel the benefit."

"Really?" I said.

"H-mm."

"Okay. You say so."

Yeah, she was trim. But she had that unhinged look in her eye. She wasn't playing with a full deck and enjoyed her crooked game. She lit a cigarette and waved it under my nose. "Want one?"

"No thanks. I have to go."

"Really? Who's waiting?" She knew the answer.

I paused. Looked her in the eye. Her insanity stared back. "You got me. What d'you want me to say? I'm going to embrace the twelve steps and let God into my life and everything will be okay?"

"If you say so."

"What?"

"Honey, if you came here for the cure I got news for you. There ain't no cure. Just we got to deal with it and keep rolling on down the highway."

I laughed. It unnerved her.

"What?" she asked.

I pointed in through the open doors to the hall we had just left. "Those assholes in there, those fucking wastes of skin, they're just a denialist support group. Each one tells the guy next to him it's fine to blame everything on their old man or mom. Bullshit."

"You're cured." She snapped her fingers. I laughed again, this time with her. She hacked her smokers cough and leaned on me to clear her throat. I held her shoulder. "Say, Rudy, that's your name right?" I nodded agreement, "Seeing as you got the cure, how'd you like to join me for a cocktail? My treat. I like a man who makes me laugh."

I figured it wouldn't hurt. "You know what? Fuck it. Come on princess. My car or yours?"

Marcy smiled. "I wasn't thinking that far ahead" She smelled the air close to me. I held my breath. "I guess we could take your car." Her eyes glinted.

We drove a couple of blocks to a bar we were both vaguely familiar with. She drank cosmopolitans and I had beer. She was a riot. Everything was a sexual innuendo with her. She spent the first hour building me up and then taking me down, then asking if I had a large penis. She'd do the same time after time, each round ending with a different question about my body, my preferences, or experiences. Did I shave my balls? Do I like threesomes? Have I ever been restrained?

Can I remember the name of every woman I've slept with? I avoided most questions but I guess she could tell I was excited. I drew the line when she asked me if I'd let a woman fuck me up the ass with a strap-on. My whole body contracted. She asked the question just as the young waitress collected our empty glasses. The waitress looked up at me, her eyes seemingly saying 'would you?'.

"Same again guys?" the waitress asked.

"Hell yeah!" Marcy said loudly. A few people turned to see who the loud-mouth was. "So?" She asked me. The waitress winked as she turned on her heels back to the bar.

"What the..." I was dumbstruck. Marcy had beat me into a pulp. "Who cares. It's not like I'm really going to have to face the option, is it?"

"I don't know. You tell me." she smiled.

I got up and went to the rest-room. When I returned we had fresh drinks and Marcy had written something on a piece of paper she had torn out of her journal. It was a web address for a meetup.com group.

"What the fuck is this?"

"Sign up. When you do, I'll get a message. I'm a member. I'll be your buddy. It's a lot of fun. Like pyramid selling."

"What kind of group is it?"

She flicked her eyebrows.

"Look, I'm not into the whole swinging thing. If you need to get laid just ask."

Marcy burst out laughing. She fell off her stool. "It's nothing like that. Your buddy makes sure you have a good time is all."

"What's in it for you?"

She dusted herself off and leaned in close, "Honey, some of us like to have pleasure and some of us like to give pleasure. I'm a giver."

"Okay. That... makes perfect sense."

She laughed at my sarcasm. "Let's get drunk." I ordered a whiskey.

"Sounds good." She ordered a Mai Tai and two shots of Jim Beam. I complained about Jim Beam not being real whiskey. She told me that it didn't matter and that I wasn't going to get to fuck her. She said it as if there was a slim chance I might, and it drove me wild. Instant hard-on. Like I was fifteen again. She smiled. She knew what was happening in my mind. She'd been toying with me all night. For the first time in years, I had enjoyed myself, really enjoyed myself.

We got drunk. A few drinks later she flashed me during a fit of giggles we got ourselves in. One guy who caught the whole thing on his way out of the bar called her a whore. She just said 'yup' as she tucked her tits back into her blouse and fastened the top button.

I woke up the next morning on my sofa again, still dressed. Marcy's note was on the coffee table with my billfold and cell phone. I checked the time using my cell. It was ten fifty in the morning. I had one text message. It was from Marcy. I didn't remember putting her number in my contacts. The message was simple. It said 'thnks 4 a blast!'

I called her cell. It went straight to voice-mail. While the instructions played I cleared my throat. "Hi Marcy. Rudy. Got your message." I paused. "Call me and we'll hook up again." I ended the call. I scratched my balls and pulled my pants from out of my ass.

I got up and waddled into the kitchen to make coffee. I figured a hit of caffeine would be good to get my bowels moving and numb the aches that seemed to be all over my body. I was about to pour coffee when my cell rang. Thinking it would be Marcy I stumbled into the lounge onto the sofa. It wasn't her. "Hey."

"You sound like shit."

"Sven. Fuck, I thought you were someone else."

"Nice. Hey, what you got going today? I have an opening in my schedule and wondered if you'd like to come over, help me fill it?"

Sven had been a long-time buddy. In the time we'd known each other I hadn't been able to figure how he funded his lifestyle. He never had a job but he always had money. He didn't sell drugs. I'd stuck close to him for a whole week once and he never had anything dangerous in his hand except a bottle of Bud Light when the bar we were in ran out of Negra Modelo. He figured Bud Light didn't taste of anything so it wouldn't take the taste of Negra away.

I drove over to his house in Echo Park and we set to working on a couple of bottles of scotch. He had an 18-year-old Jameson and a bottle of Crown Royal. We switched drinks every round. We sat in the front yard of his place, basking in the sun while we drank the day away.

Sven's joint wasn't much but it was his – bought and paid for. I'd had a key to it for as long as I can remember but never used it because there was always some degenerate using the place as a crash pad. A guy called Tony rented a room from Sven. Tony was a slippery motherfucker but he had known Sven longer than me so I let it ride.

We got to talking and I told him about the website Marcy told me about. He said he'd heard of it. He'd heard it was a scam to get dirt on people and blackmail them. I didn't go for the blackmail angle. I had nothing worth stealing and I had no money. What would be the point? Sven said it was a power thing. Some people need to control other people, one of them wanted to control me.

"Who knows. I mean, she was a great girl." I said, breaking a silence in the late afternoon.

"What?"

"Marcy. She had a great body."

"Toss her out your mind. She'll rot your brain and ruin your life. You know what you need?"

"What's that?"

"To unload your wad on some bitch."

"Whatever. You sound like her."

"I'm serious. You should do that young girl in the apartment next to yours."

"Get outta town. She wouldn't let me in the door!"

"She's hot though. In that plain way."

"What?"

"She's interestingly ugly. I bet she's dirty. I bet you couldn't fuck her within a month."

"I know I couldn't."

"Okay then, I bet you couldn't do the old maid in the other apartment. The one with the snake."

"Even if I could I'm not going to. She's fuckin' nuts man."

"That's my point. Makes the little hottie seem easier, don't it?"

I mixed Jameson and Crown Royal and held it up, "A King James!" I downed the tumbler full of whiskey and grimaced. "No. Not really."

"I'll put a grand down. Ten big ones." he smiled.

"To fuck the girl?"

"Both."

"No way, man."

"One thousand dollars Rudy, one thousand dollars. That's the offer, right there, kemosabe."

"Okay. I'll give it a go."

"I need photographic evidence of the carnal event, King James."

I shook my head. I knew what was coming. Realisation hit. "How fucking stupid am I?"

Sven pulled his battered old snub nose out of his cargo-shorts and cocked it. "If you don't I'll shoot your pinky toe." He leaned forward and held the gun over my left foot and smiled up into my face. "We have a deal?"

"Okay. Put the gun away. You're a fucking liability."

He spun the thing around in the air like some delusional gay Mexican cowboy coming out in front of the pope. It was old and looked like it had seen heavy duty action.

"You ever shot that?"

He shrugged, held it straight above him, pointing to the sky and fired two rounds.

"Asshole!" I leapt from my seat and dived for cover through the kitchen door. He remained on his chair laughing. I have no idea where the bullets landed. "You could have shot me!" I yelled.

"I know. Pussy. I didn't though, did I?"

There was always the risk Sven would do something crazy if you went drinking with him. His face dropped and his mood did the same, like the wind had blown the cheer right out of him. "Don't you have women to fuck?"

His bite and malice cut the air. I left and drove home taking the back roads, mainly driving down alleys because I was pretty sure any cop within a five-block radius would be able to smell my breath.

Things got so bad that by the second month of having no regular cash flow I decided I would apply to every conceivable vacancy in the LA Weekly. I circled twenty-three jobs I figured I could manage to do. I got six interviews for the following week and a letter from the landlord asking where last month's rent was so I bought a dress shirt, some slacks and a new razor. On the upside, Sven let the bet slide so technically I was a thousand dollars and a little toe better off.

The last interview from a day of rejections was for a record store. When I walked in two thirds of the kids stopped what they were doing and looked at me. A handful left, pushing past me on their way out. They didn't even give me chance to get out of the entrance. Bemused, I headed to the counter. Before I could ask for the manager, the kid working the checkout confronted me.

"You a cop? We haven't done nothing, sir."

The kids in the store were still staring at me, those who had decided to stick around that is.

"Is this Sonic Sounds?"

"Yeah..." the kid said.

Another kid with bad dress sense and oily skin stepped up beside the one I was speaking to. Two gazelles wondering if the big lion in front of them had eaten dinner yet. I looked around the store at the t-shirts and clothes, the comic books, the skateboard junk hanging off the walls and the shelves of CDs and random vinyl.

"What's with all the junk. I thought this was a music store."

"Sir, we sell a lifestyle. How can I help you?"

"I'd like to see the manager."

"Dude, you are a cop, aren't you?!"

"No. Do I look like one?" The asshole just gave me that teenage angst thing; hands out in my direction in a mental 'need I say anymore' gesture. "Look, I'm not a cop". I leaned in closer to the counter and used a low voice. I have no idea why. It was a natural thing to do it seemed.

"If you say so. You kinda look like one."

"You from trading standards?" his buddy asked, still half hiding behind the first pimply stick insect.

"You got something to hide?"

You could practically see their assholes bite down on their vintage jeans. We used to call those things second hand or, more accurately, we used to call them trash. Kids these days call them vintage if they have light soiling, and antique if they are damaged and completely fucking obscure to the tune of three decades. While they squirmed, I continued talking.

"Look, my name's Rudy Whitman and I'm here to see the manager."

"That's Martin. He's the manager." The pimply one pointed to the anaemic one behind him.

"Well, Martin the Manager, I'm here for my interview."

"You're Rudy?"

"Tada!" I held my hands out. It blew their minds.

"You want to work here?"

"No, I need a job and you have one going. Anyways I like music."

A kid behind me snorted in disgust at my comment. I glared at him. He put down the CD and moved along a couple of feet before randomly picking up whatever was in front of him to hide his nerves. I smiled at Martin. He was obviously running a million thoughts through his mind. One kid near the counter stepped up and raised a hand to high-five me.

"Does this look like the set of Back To The Future to you?" I said. I shook my head. He fucked off.

"I'm sorry, there's been some confusion," Martin stammered, "We assumed you were, you know, our age when you called earlier."

"No son, I'm more mature, like the women you jack off to."

"Why d'you want a job here?

"Look, I'm a pap. Paparazzo. I shoot people doing shit they shouldn't and sell the pictures but this whole internet thing has fucked me. I figure the only thing the internet can't fuck up is music. And I know my shit about good music."

"Do you know who Armand Van Helding is?"

"Was he a Nazi war criminal? Is this a fascist test?"

"He's a DJ from Europe. He's massive in New York. I don't think this is the right job for you."

"Okay, I see it." For some reason I liked Martin. He was young but he hadn't flinched once. "Try this one on fuckers, name the first major band Joe Walsh was in."

"Who the hell is Joe Walsh?" the high-fiver asked.

"You say I don't know music? Joe fucking Walsh. Guitar legend." They all looked blank. "The Eagles?"

"The Eagles," Martin nodded confidently.

"No, dipshit, I asked what was his first major band."

"Oh."

I looked at them in turn for someone who had heard the rumour that music had existed before 1998. I was on my own. "The James Gang."

A small voice from somewhere in the back of the store piped up: "Wasn't that an outlaw gang? I saw that movie last year." I died a little on the inside.

"Look, Martin, I think you're right. This isn't the place for me. Thanks for your time." I turned to leave. On the way out I yelled to the pipsqueak at the rear. "The James Gang was Joe Walsh's band before he joined The Eagles, asshole! Some people consider the work he did in that band to be better than that he did in The Eagles. Inflammatory, I know, but there you have it."

A few stunned faces tracked me as I left the store. I think Martin's buddy shit himself a little.

I had just about hauled my fat ass across the sidewalk when I heard the door open.

"If you want it, the job's yours." Martin was holding the door open, staring at me. The kid had a pair on him. I stopped, turned, pawed my hair back from my face and squinted in the sun like a vampire on day release.

"Come again? Why me?"

"Basic economics. We've got a rock section at the back that needs love. You're the only person who's mentioned rock music. It's either you, or we don't sell a whole bunch of CDs. And that will cost more than paying you to work here. If there was another way, I'd take it. If you're serious, the job's yours. Two-week trial."

"Fuck it, Martin. Yeah, why not?"

"You start tomorrow. We open at eight thirty."

"Who the fuck buys music before noon?"

"Your choice." He looked at me for a moment. "See you tomorrow, Rudy." He gave me one last look and let the door close behind him leaving me on the sidewalk.

"Fuck. Eight thirty." I drove to Erica's apartment. She'd just be getting home.

HIGHLY
COMMENDED

GUILT, BY ADAM KENDALL
CHAPTER – COBURG, VIC

ONE

Whack!

For a pillow, that hurt pretty bad. She really swung it with some force. Why is she cranky at me? I'm a good person. Aren't I?

"Hrmph..." comes my exhaled reply, muffled by my pillow. From the way my head and neck are stuck, I've been crammed in the same position since I went to bed. Shit, what's the time? What time did I get home last night?

Last night... oh god, she didn't swing the pillow really hard at me, it's my head that hurts, not the pillow. "I'm sorry" I manage to drool out of my mouth, as I unsuccessfully try and lift my head to open my eyes.

"You're bloody sorry are you? And what exactly for?"

I don't know what I'm sorry for. But if you feel the way I'm feeling right now, surely you've done something terrible. I've gotta try and get my eyes open and sort myself out. I just can't seem to manage it because my head feels like it's being held down by a lead blanket.

She's starting up again. "Are you sorry for coming home at three am? Or for me having to let you in because you couldn't get your key in the front door?" I can't even manage to brace myself for this verbal onslaught I can feel building.

"Or are you sorry for stinking of booze—and bloody perfume? Or for boring the shit out of me at three am by telling me over and over again how great a mate Mick is to you?"

She's silently yelling at me through gritted teeth so the kids don't hear.

"Maybe you're sorry for tripping over your own feet in the hallway and waking half the fucking house up!"

I don't remember any of that. At least now I know what time I got home. Three am, really?! The fact I can't remember getting home at that time, or how I got home means it must've been a boozy affair. Come on, I need to retrace my steps. Where was I?

The Livingstone Arms. I got there before Mick and sat at the front bar. It was busy, but not packed and I ordered a pint. Mick got there about half way into my second pint. We ordered a counter meal. Closing time, midnight.

Blank hours and moments where I could've been anywhere, been anyone and done anything. I must've been pretty shit-faced because I haven't had a drunken memory loss for well over 2 years. I hate it when this happens. It honestly scares the shit out of me because I get this awful feeling that I'll end up being hauled away on charges of assault or some weird crime where I can't honestly remember what took place, but someone's security camera has caught me at the front of their house trying to make love to their letter box or something.

Would I do that, or could I be that kind of person? No, I don't think so. But I can NEVER confirm it unless I absolutely remember everything that happened. So, maybe I could be that kind of person. Why, for example, do I smell like perfume? I would never be unfaithful, it just isn't in my DNA, but now I'm extremely paranoid.

I lean over and smell my shirt. It does smell of perfume.

A shoulder, with a crisp white shirt. I'm leaning.
There's no attraction. Sadness.

Whack! That paranoia is quickly pulled into check by something else she's thrown at me while she's getting ready for work. My eyes are glued shut, they ain't coming open for a little while at least, so I'm not sure what she's flung at me this time.

I can hear her pulling her stockings up, fixing her shirt and tucking it into her stockings (just like an old lady does, she hates it when I say that). Now I can hear her putting a top on, doing the buttons up. My eyes just can't open yet, it all hurts too much right now. She's quickly stepping into a skirt,—zip goes the back of the skirt. Then I wait for the familiar sound of her favourite work boots. Schloop, zip, left boot done. Schloop, zip, right boot done. She's dressed.

"And what's the story with you crying yourself to sleep?"

"Wait, what?" I say as I raise my head.

Uncontrollable sadness was seeping from my every pore. Trying to
hold myself upright while ordering an Uber. I had to get home.

"You sobbed and sobbed until you fell asleep."

"I'm sorry, I was just really pissed." I reply. None of this is getting any better.

"Ernest you need to get up, for fuck's sake! I have that meeting we spoke about and you need to take the kids to school. Remember?!"

"OK, I'm sorry Linda, I'm up... Yep I remember." I'm lying, I don't remember talking about taking the kids to school today, however I don't think now is the time to bring that up (or anything else for that matter). I have a fair bit of crawling to do to get out of this one. I just need to remember where I was and what actually happened before I work on my crawling strategy.

"The boys and I will ride to school. All good..." I start to say as I swing both legs over the side of the bed. I attempt to roll over and stand up, but fall off the bed, ever so ungraciously. Thump! This really drives home the point to both Linda and I that I am clearly still hammered.

"You are not taking our children on their bikes. You're still pissed! You'll end up in an accident. Just forget it, I'll just have to be late to my meeting."

The meeting. Yes, I remember now. I am taking the kids to school because of the meeting. She has been talking to me about how important this meeting is for over a month. How her boss's boss will be there and it's her opportunity to show the good work she's been doing. And she has been doing good work, she's been working her ass off. Skipping sitting-up and binge watching our favourite TV shows because she's been so passionate about making an impact at work. Long nights, early mornings, and passion-fuelled stress, not the kind of stress that you get when you're worrying about nothing. The kind of stress that comes with good, hard work where you really want to achieve. I can't let her down, not today. Not today.

"No no no..." I'm kneeling on the floor after trying to right myself. Falling out of bed, still drunk is not the start to the day my wife needs, when I should be totally under control and just take care of life stuff so she can kick goals at work.

I manage to get onto my feet and steady myself. "It's all good. I'll have a shower, eat some toast, get the boys fed and dressed and we'll get an Uber, we'll be fine." I do a good job of trying to convince myself that I can actually make it to the shower and stomach some toast, let alone find my phone so I can order the Uber.

"Are you OK mate?"

Why would the Uber driver ask me that? What was my answer?
Why was I upset on my way home last night?

"What's the time?" I ask as I'm checking the bedside clock. It's only 7:25AM. "You go to your meeting. I've got this. The boys and I have time to get ready and get an Uber."

Now she's just staring at me. I can tell by the look on her face that this is a solution that will work and that she has to accept my offer. I've only just scraped through though. She's still so cranky at me that she just walks away in acceptance, rather than giving me a verbal reply or looking at me.

TWO

"Bye boys, have a great day." says Linda as she's heading out the front door.

"Bye mum!" Julian says, all dressed and ready for school.

"See ya..." Ricky manages to blurt out, while he's still at the kitchen bench in his pjs, stuffing his fifth or sixth wheat bix in his mouth. For a ten year old kid who's built like a ladder, he eats as though he plays front row prop for the Wallabies. Our fruit bowl is never full enough and his stomach is a machine that just keeps needing to be fed.

These mornings are a constant. No matter what war is raging in which continent, as long as it's not here, there will be two kids who are at times polar opposites to each other. There will forever be the dreaded positive reinforcement of eating breakfast, brushing teeth, getting dressed and stop arguing with your brother, until it's down to the wire to get to school on time.

"Finished your breakfast mate?" I ask Ricky as he's finishing up. I can't look at his food as I think I'll vomit. I'm holding onto the kitchen bench, riding the latest wave of morning-after alcohol-induced nausea.

"Yep."

"What about you Julian?"

"Nah, not hungry" he whines.

"Oh, come on mate," I plead as I'm resting my head on the bench "you've got to eat your brekkie."

"You haven't Dad. You're still in your pjs."

He's right, I am still in my pjs and I can't bear the thought of food at the moment.

"I'm going for a shower. I expect you to at least have eaten something when I get out, OK?"

"OK."

He won't have eaten anything, and I'd usually get extremely agitated because he can't do the simplest of things, like eat his bloody breakfast. It normally ends up with me getting flustered to the point where we end up arguing about it and we still get to the same result. "Pick your battles," I hear Linda saying to me "he's only seven." She's so patient with the kids.

No need to pick anything this morning because I'm presented with only one battle, and that's dealing with this hangover and the dreadful feeling I have in my core due to large parts of last night missing from my memory.

Warm water covers me over, from head to foot, finding its way around every piece of me, washing away the filth blocking my pores with last night's pints and god knows whatever else. This is the best I've felt since I woke up, lost in the flow of water trickling over me, away from the mess in the kitchen and the kids who aren't dressed or haven't eaten yet. I can forget about being an adult for five minutes and just be here. I close my eyes and lean my head against the cold tiles in the shower.

Crisp white shirt. Perfume. Citrus and vanilla. "Shh. Come on now, they'll be OK, and so will you. You'll just need to work through it..."

Who was she? She? Why was she telling me that? Why was I leaning on her?

I snap back into the white noise and movement of the water falling from the shower head, opening my eyes and they get filled with water. I slap the shower tiles in frustration and it hurts my hand. I need to remember what I did last night! Why was I leaning on a woman, with a white shirt?

Feeling unsettled by my wandering mind and feeling sick at what it vaguely reminded of what I had done, I quickly turn the shower off and grab my towel. I'm drying myself so quickly I feel the burn on my skin from my favourite rough old towel.

"Are you dressed Ricky?" I shout from out of the bathroom.

"Yes Dad, stop hassling me!"

"Alright, good boy."

THREE

As we're out the front of the house waiting for the Uber to take us to school, I hear and feel my stomach grumble, and I regret not eating. I would pay a lot of money right now for a can of coke and a bacon and egg role. I'd never hear the end of it from the kids; all the sugar in the coke, all the fat in the bacon. But it'd sure as hell be one way to cure this hangover.

"Still not here." Julian says as he's tracking the driver with my phone.

I pull the front door closed behind us and push against the door to make sure it's definitely locked. I push it again, to double check, as I always do. I can't help it. I know I locked it the first time, but I always need to double check. I do the same with the back door before I go to bed at night.

I feel nauseous again and lean against the railing that wraps around our front porch. It wobbles under my weight and reminds me that I never got around to fixing it properly. I only got a half-arsed job done the first time because I just couldn't handle another trip to Bunnings, down aisle eleven where all the fixings are and waiting for some person who works there to help me understand that I have no idea about what I am doing.

So many things to fix in these 1950s built brick-veneer homes, except for the bricks; they're as sturdy as the day they were laid. All of these homes really similar in style and build on this street, but the years have afforded them their uniqueness and individual charm. Our house makes its mark with my keeping-up-with-the-Joneses-perfect lawn and edges, married suitably with Linda's two prize winning rose bushes. Well, I consider them prize winning, she hasn't actually ever entered them into any contest. I admire her determination and care on those two plants, and they get so many comments from neighbours and passers-by.

"Come on Dad!" Ricky screams at me while holding the door to the Uber open. When did that get here?

I hop in the back of the Uber with the kids and put my seatbelt on. I reach over and help Ricky with his seatbelt. Julian's already locked and loaded. He loves to do things himself and especially when it comes to safety matters. I swear he'll be an OH&S representative at where ever he works. Maybe a public health inspector.

It's hot and stuffy in here and I wind the window down, hoping the cool air will shock me out of how I'm feeling.

"Do you want the window down mate?"

"Sure," I said "what.. (hiccup.... burp) ... what evers is, isss easier."

"Just don't spew OK, you're nearly home."

"Nah mate, I'm orwright."

I wasn't going to spew, but I wasn't alright either. Sobbing at three AM in a bloody Uber.

Opening my eyes helps me snap back into now. I watch the houses rush by as we sit in school traffic. I then stare intently into the driver's rear view mirror, trying to see if I recognise him. Was he my driver from last night? Can he fill me in and tell me if I was a good person? Can he tell me why the hell I was sobbing?

It's not him. No help.

"Let's go!" Ricky is out of the Uber like lightning, bag dragging along the ground as he's running for the gate.

Julian isn't so eager. In the mornings, he says he's always bored at school and doesn't want to go. Then in the afternoons you can't shut him up about what a great day he's had and how much he's learned.

I slowly get out of the car like a wounded bull, groan as I stand up straight and close the door gently.

"Thanks mate" I manage to mumble as he drives off. I'll give him five stars later. Not sure why, but it's just how it is these days, isn't it?

I walk inside the school gate, watching all the perfect parents who didn't ply themselves with loads of grog last night. Watching how they're all fresh and bubbly, chatting to each other before the bell rings for all the kids to go inside. Watching all the kids run manic, kicking balls to each other, tugging on each other shirts or playing tiggy or tag or whatever you call it from the state you're from. I manage to dodge a few people I normally say hello to so they can't smell my breath or notice exactly how poorly I am right now. I'm already feeling terrible enough, like I've let my wife down on a really important day, I don't want all the judging parents to think I'm also a terrible father.

I'm standing in that school yard and the place turns into an amphitheatre of white noise. I feel a cold sweat start to bead on every part of my face, neck and head. Oh Jesus Christ, not here, not now. I begin to swallow, over and over again.

RRRRIIIIIIINNNNNNNGGGGGG

Oh thank you! The bell.

"See ya Dad!"

"Bye Dad..."

Both the boys come and give me a hug and run off to their classes. I manage to mumble something to them along the lines of "See you, love you... pick you up this after..." and I walk as quickly as I can for the front gate.

I make it to the gate, my vision getting blurry. I feel like I'm going to faint. Beads of cold sweat pouring down my neck and my hands are so clammy. I manage to stumble and trip out the front gate, onto the nature strip, grab onto a tree and hug it like a giant who has come to my rescue. I can't see for all the stars in my eyes and I lean forward and to the side of the tree. I feel my glasses fall off my face and onto the ground and then it happens… I vomit and make the most god-awful wrenching sound as spew pours out of my mouth and onto the ground with that unmistakable splashing sound.

"Oh… thank fuck for that" I say as I begin to instantly feel better and wipe spew and saliva from my mouth and onto the sleeve of my shirt.

My vision comes back and my shirt is wet from all the sweat. I look around and there are two groups of mothers just staring at me, mouths open. One of them is holding the leash of her labradoodle and holding it back from my spew. It's trying to jump forward to lick it up I suppose, but being caught each time by the collar on its neck. I just want to kick the bloody dog and take out my embarrassment on the poor furry mutt, but I don't have the energy or the will.

I lift my head and turn back and the Principal in his office at the front of the school looking out his window in amazement, at what has just happened. Another parent, a Dad, comes past and clearly feels for me. He's the only one moving and he walks straight up to me and says "Are you OK mate?"

"Are you OK mate?" Mick says. "Look I know it's a lot, but Trish… you know… she's great and all… and I know you've been friends for life… Look I know she's been part of your life for ever…"

Trish. Trish was the one wearing the white crisp shirt. Trish is the smell of perfume. Of course, it all makes sense now. Like a flash through the blackest storm clouds, I've managed to piece it all back together. Only this time there's no rain of sobbing, just a wave of pale washing over my face; the pure shock of remembering exactly just what happened last night. Finally. If it wasn't so bad, I'd be rejoicing at the fact I can finally remember it all. Instead I hold onto that tree that's stopping me from face planting into my own vomit, and I just let out a sigh. "Urgh..."

I stare at the ground. Any other person who is there at this point in time is now out of my conscious and I am completely immersed with the emotions of what happened last night. I am not at peace, but I am at acceptance. Finally, it has come through and my worst fears have been realised, like a reflection from an old dirty mirror that I should never have brought out of the shed and wiped down.

"Hey mate, are you OK?" The other parent asks again.

I pull my head around, and it takes half a second for the earth to follow.

"Yeah, I'm alright." And I am alright this time. But only just alright. I'm a husband, and a father, and I need to start acting like that. I need to lift myself up and out of this mess and face into what happened last night. I owe it to myself and the kids, at the very least.

I look around at all the judging, perfect, bubbly parents. Those who have never stepped a wrong foot in their lives and have their perfect houses and barbecues and fine wines with six figure salaries and endless nights of romance with their partners, amazing kids who clean up after themselves and are top of their class and aren't being stretched enough in school work and fit right in and are in the school bloody football team. They're wives and husbands who are just right for each other and they skip along trulalalah to where ever they fucking go each day while their dog sits at the back door obediently and doesn't make a sound because he's a perfect poochy woochy... who's a good boy?!

Fuck them. I pick my glasses up out of the grass and shake the vomit off. I lift my head and look around slowly at all the judging faces, and I walk off.

FOUR

"Ernest!" Linda calls out as she is walking in the front door. "Boys!?"

I'm standing in the kitchen, with my eyes shut, letting the late afternoon sun hit my eye lids, trying to remain emotionless and keep my composure so I can just get this over with. I take a deep breath, "I'm in here." I call back.

Linda walks confidently into the kitchen, plonking her bags on the bench. She has a smile on her face and a spring in her step. "So are you going to ask me how I went today? I smashed it! They absolutely loved me. Graham, you know, my bosses boss, well he was just full of praise and was really impressed. I mean REALLY impressed. All that hard work has paid off and I think they're going to move forward with my recommendations. Well most of them at least..."

I try to interrupt her flow. "I think we need to chat..."

"Yeah OK, sure." She says as she opens the fridge. "Is there any wine open?"

I try to get a word in again, but she continues "So I'll have to do a bit more work on the project, but not as much as I have been doing, and I think it might even lead to a promotion if I play my cards right..."

"We need to chat..." I managed to mumble.

"Sure. Should we celebrate? Where are the boys? Boys?!"

"Linda for fuck's sake! Sit down, please." I'm shaking.

"Umm... OK. Are you OK? Where are the kids?" Linda slowly starts to take a seat at the kitchen bench.

"The boys are around at Mike and Graham's playing with the other kids. Look Linda, we need to talk."

She's frowning, staring at me. Her pure joy and excitement of a clearly awesome day at work has been completely sapped out of her. "Christ, what's wrong Ernest?"

I pause, swallow a few times and take a seat near her. I can't look her in the eye, but I manage to. "You know how I went out with Mick last night?"

"Yeah, so?"

"Well Trish came out as well. So I think the perfume you smelt was, Trish. Anyway, Trish found out that I was out having a drink with Mick and she came out especially and met us...." My head is spinning and I'm finding this extremely difficult. I'm skipping around trying to blurt out as many facts about the night as I can, making up for all the memory loss I had today. I don't know if I'm skipping around the point or trying to get to it quickly.

"OK. So Trish was there, great. She's been one of your best friends for years. So what? What are you saying Ernest?"

"Well she was telling me how... she had been out on the town the other week and she was going to call me... well she..." I feel like I'm going to vomit again.

"Get to the point Ernest, you're scaring me!" Tears are now filling both of our eyes. We're both an absolute mess and we've only been at it for a minute.

I stop talking, and take out my phone. I unlock it using my P.I.N. because face ID isn't working. Maybe I look unrecognisable with so many tears running down my cheeks? I open my messages from Trish and push the phone across the bench. Linda looks down at the phone. She stares at the photo of Trish I have opened on my phone, where

Trish is out in a bar with one of her mates, shots of something in hand, taking a selfie. They're both clearly having a great time.

"Ernest, so what? Why am I looking a photo of Trish and some other woman I don't know?"

I take the phone back, my fingers trembling uncontrollably. After the third attempt, I manage to zoom in on the photo. I zoom in on the background of the photo, where I can see behind Trish and her mate, a dark booth where there's drinks on a table. It's dark and a little blurry, but you can see it alright. Sitting at the booth behind Trish and her mate is a woman, and a tall smartly dressed guy who is sitting on the same side of the booth as her, and she is leaning in against him, they're almost spooning, but sitting down. She is up against him and looking behind herself, straight into his face. She's staring into his eyes and he is holding her around the middle. They both look so happy. He's holding her, half across her breasts, and half across her middle. They are staring at each other like they are either about to kiss, or have just done so. It's almost a kitsch movie poster, like it's staged or rehearsed.

The woman in the photo is clearly Linda. I have no idea who the guy is.

"I didn't know how to tell you Ernie. You're one of my best friends."

Trish. She's always been there for me, along with Mick. Through thick and thin.

Linda picks the phone up and just stares at it. She looks at the moment captured. The moment that is the catalyst for our lives being turned upside down. The moment where my utter devotion to her for over twenty years has been thrown back in my face.

She puts the phone down and looks nervously around the room. Tears streaming now. Short sharp breaths. Her face changes again as her eyebrows peak in the middle, brow furrowed and her lips are trembling.

A look of pure guilt.

THE BATTLE OF BARBER STREET, BY JIM BLACK
CHAPTER – PASCOE VALE, VIC

Karl hurled himself over the low wall, the bullets chasing him like angry wasps.

"Did you think that looked cool?" asked Fish, already leaning against the wall with his duct tape out, "because you didn't. You looked like a three-legged dog getting pushed down the stairs."

"Shut up, Fish," said Karl. Fish had his speed dealers on, but Karl could tell he was rolling his eyes. The battle cries of the Barber Street boys carried from down the street, punctuated by impacts on the other side of the wall. Red dust drifted down. He heard one of the projectiles strike the letterbox and ricochet around inside, rattling like a donation tin.

The wall radiated hot against his back. The ochre render trapped and spilled the sweltering summer heat like a leaky bucket. The wall stood slightly higher where Fish was sitting, a slope in the grass giving him more protection. Karl crawled over, careful to keep his head low. "I need another balloon," he said.

"What, you're through them all already?"

"I dropped the bag!"

"Course you did," Fish said, but he handed over a balloon, and, after a moment, the duct tape. Karl ripped the old balloon off and hastily set about applying the new one. Blue wasn't the luckiest colour, but better to be armed unluckily than not armed at all.

It had gone quiet beyond the wall, the hot stillness of midday summer. Everything smelled like lavender bushes, burning fuel, cooked dogshit. Somewhere nearby a crow cawed. Karl and Fish looked at each other. "Not like them to give up so easily," said Karl.

"It's probably lunchtime. Where the fuck are Beth and Patio, anyway?"

Karl wasn't sure how to answer that without looking like an idiot. The crow cawed again. He could see it, sitting on the Stobie pole. Just waiting for us all to stop mucking around, no doubt. "I always reckon they're saying my name."

"What?"

"The crows. You know. 'Karl, Karl, Karl.'"

Fish looked at him for a moment, then thumped him hard in the shoulder.

"Ow! Hey!"

"What the fuck is wrong with you, mate? Don't answer that, I don't actually want to know. Where are Beth and Patio? Answer that one, Karl, that one I care about."

Karl rubbed his shoulder. "We got separated."

"No shit. Look, either tell me now or I'll get the whole story from Beth when she rocks up."

"She—" No way to say it without sounding like an idiot. "The Barber Street Boys, they...they had a flame-thrower."

Even the crow was silent at that. After a moment Fish asked, "What, like a can of deodorant and a lighter?"

"Nah, man," said Karl, feeling much older than his eleven years, "it was flash as. Can't you smell it?"

The smell of burning was strong, obvious now that it was pointed out. He watched the doubt creep over Fish's skinny face.

"Like, a real one?" asked Fish, but Karl just shrugged. The older boy picked up his rifle. "And...what. They cooked her? And Patio too?"

"Nah, nah!" said Karl, "they're fine, I think. We were heading to Morley's shed, because Patio reckons you can see straight into the Barber Street backyards from the roof. But I dropped my bag and went back to get it, and they shot the thing between us. They didn't burn her, or Patio, I'm sure of it. They're not that dumb."

"It's forty degrees today, playing with fire is pretty fucking dumb," Fish said, but he looked relieved at the thought that the others weren't immolated. The rifles the boys held were just PVC pipes, with balloons duct taped to one end to make a slingshot. Not much of a weapon against an actual goddamn flame-thrower.

Fish risked a quick peek over the wall. "Reckon they've cleared out. Come on, let's get out of here."

They left the yard, crossing the purple carpet of jacaranda blossoms and keeping a close eye out for any of the Barber Street kids. To get back to the base without crossing any of the usual battlegrounds meant a dash across the intersection, holding their breath past the witch lady's overgrown house, race around the corner with the big bottlebrush, past the place with the half dozen junk cars in the front yard, and then through the driveway and over the fence of the old Indian bloke, Mr Rajagopalan. He didn't move from in front of the cricket on his old-school TV, but he watched them sprint over the oven-hot concrete and clamber over the wooden fence posts. Then down the alley, setting off all the dogs, and into the Parsons' back gate.

Beth and Patio were waiting for them in the shed, soaking wet. Patio's fringe, usually reliably gelled out perpendicular to his face like the bill of a baseball cap, was plastered across his forehead. Beth was wringing her hair out, but when they banged through the hideout door, she jumped up and reached for her gun. She barely released any tension when she saw who it was. "Fish," she said, "they've got—"

"A flame-thrower, I know," said Fish, "Karl told me."

Beth turned to Karl, eyes flashing. "Oh, so you were around, hey? Just decided to scarper rather than help?"

"Beth," said Karl helplessly, "they had a flame-thrower."

"Yeah, well. Not just a flame-thrower. Show them your bruise, Patio." Patio lifted his wet shirt. Beneath his collarbone was a huge red welt, the size of a fist.

"Jesus," whispered Fish, tugging at his mullet anxiously. Karl felt a little sick. They'd all been shot before, of course, but the little pellets rarely left bruises larger than a five-cent piece. This was new.

"They've got some machine thing," squeaked Patio in his high-pitched voice, "fires out tennis balls, but, like, super-fast. I didn't even have time to move, like. That fat kid, Jackson, he carried it round like a bazooka."

"We had to jump from the shed into Farquharson's pool to get away," said Beth.

"Fucking thing had just been chlorinated, like. Farquharson puts too much of that shit in, my eyes are stinging like anything."

"Yeah, you look like shit," said Fish, "even more than usual, I mean."

This started a small scuffle that only ended when Beth hit the corrugated wall of the hideout with her gun. "That's enough," she said, and the boys immediately broke apart. "Why are they changing things now? Where are they even getting the money for this stuff? It's a big jump from balloons and pipes to flame-throwers and grenade launchers. None of them kids has a job. And who'd sell that stuff to kids anyway? So where's it coming from? And why are they changing things?" She grabbed her bag and swung it onto her shoulder. "I need to go and think about this. Stay out of sight and we'll meet back here tomorrow." She looked around at each of them, saw the fear in her eyes, and scowled. "We're going to win, fellas, alright? We'll work this out. The Gilchrist Street Army doesn't back down!" She banged out the shed, disappearing into the glare of the summer sun.

Patio, Fish and Karl looked at each other. "See you tomorrow then, I guess," said Karl, and slunk away.

The second day of the battle went worse.

Karl was sitting on the cinder-block wall that ran between the alley and Barber Street houses. He was supposed to be spying on the Barber Street boys' base and working out where they were getting all this new gear from, but he was distracted by Mr Farquharson pouring yet more chlorine into his pool.

Mr Farquharson was the most freckled person Karl had ever seen. His head had no hair to speak of except a bristly black moustache, going grey in stripes. Between the freckles and the striped moustache, Karl couldn't shake the idea that he was some sort of mélange of African animals far from home, a leopard skin man with a zebra moustache, an impression strengthened with his strong accent.

Despite Farquharson's best efforts, the pool seemed greener today than yesterday. Karl watched the man's freckled pate shine in the sun as he disappeared back inside the house. The smell of the chlorine and the heat of the day were overpowering. Perhaps that's why Karl didn't notice Tiny until it was too late. Which was surprising, as Tiny was a hard kid to miss.

The Barber Street kids all seemed to be larger than the average eleven-year-old—Fish reckoned steroids, but Karl had his doubts –

and certainly larger than each member of the Gilchrist Street army, none of whom were blessed with any appreciable size. Of all the Barber Street kids, Tiny was the largest. He still played for the Rangers' Under 12s side despite numerous parental complaints; Tiny was roughly the same size and build as a road train, and about as quiet, which made it doubly disconcerting when his sudden appearance put Karl in the shade.

"Fuck!" said Karl, and fell off the wall.

Tiny was laughing. Karl scampered as best he could, but there was no cover between the wall and the pool, nowhere to hide. He raced towards the side gate, trying to zigzag. In the reflection off Mr Farquharson's French doors he saw Tiny heft a—

Jesus, a minigun?

Karl slammed through the gate as a hail of pellets chased him. Above the hammering of his heart he heard Mr Farquharson yelling in his weird accent, but he didn't stick around to listen to the lecture. Straight back across the intersection, breath racing too hard to be held past the overgrown house; he'd have to trust to luck that the gardener wouldn't nick his soul while he passed. Tiny laughed again somewhere behind him, and another storm of pellets descended. When a pellet was slung-shot out of a PVC pipe by balloon the sound was a pop and a whistle; the sound of this thing was a wasp-powered drill.

He felt the sting on his calves as Tiny found his range, a little bloom of heat, one, two, three, like bull-ant bites. He ran faster, grabbing hold of one of the branches of the old bottlebrush to skid around the corner onto Gilchrist Street and diving through the open window of one of the junked cars. The buzz-whine of the minigun had stopped; all he could hear was the sound of his heart hammering, and somewhere a crow calling out his name.

It was scorching in the car; he couldn't stay long. Karl reached up with his rifle and pushed the rear-view mirror around, trying to catch sight of Tiny without sticking anything out in the open. No sign of the Barber Street boy. He twisted his leg round to check his calf. Three ugly welts were already raised up. Karl tentatively poked one with his finger, and immediately wished he hadn't.

He carefully opened the car door and raced as quickly as he could to the base. The others were already inside, Fish holding a bag of frozen peas to his head. "If Mrs Parsons asks," said Beth before he could speak, "we were down at the nets, alright? We'll blame Toby Allen for a beamer, he's gone to the city for the week."

"Okay," said Karl, who had never in his life said more than hello to Mrs Parsons, a woman who belonged to a completely different plane of reality than her bemulleted son. "Um, Tiny had a minigun. I, uh, I don't know if I'm keen to keep playing, you know?"

"Typical," said Fish.

"Cut that out, soldiers," said Beth. She'd nicked a pair of aviators somewhere, which suited her even if they were a bit big for her face. "I don't know where they're getting this shit from, but I have a plan." She leaned forward. "And Karl, you're key to making it work."

"Oh," said Karl, unhappily. "Uh…"

"You've been watching the gardener, haven't you Karl?" He felt his cheeks burning from more than exertion. "I've seen you," said Beth, "while we're out on patrol, always one eye on the gardener's place."

"Why do you call her the gardener?" asked Patio, hair returned to its stiffened splendour. "She obviously doesn't do any fucking gardening, the house looks like it's about to be reclaimed by the bush."

"I'm not going to call her the fucking witch, am I? It'd be disrespectful."

"Plus she talks to bees," said Fish, "that's a thing gardeners do."

"What do you know about fucking gardening? You haven't even got any grass, like!" squeaked Patio, but the argument is cut short by Beth.

"Doesn't matter. The witch, then. I figure if anyone has something that'll help us turn the tide, it'll be her. And Karl, I reckon you know exactly where she's hidden her spare key. Am I right?"

Fuck, he did know exactly. Beth, always too good at reading him, saw the answer on his face.

"Alright then. Good. She's never around in the middle of the day, probably because witches do all their stuff at night. Black masses and shit. So now's the time to do it. Get her key, get inside, get something that'll win us this thing, and get back here."

"Get something?" stuttered Karl. "Like what? She's old! She's got to be in her thirties at least! She's not going to have, like, a BB gun lying round."

Beth looked at him like he was being wilfully dumb. "Karlos, she's a witch. She's got to have a magic wand or something, right? Or a big old spell book. Something will be there. She never gets busted for weed despite the whole joint smelling like a music festival, she's obviously got some magic that's scared the coppers into leaving her alone."

The cops aren't after her because she's a white woman with her own house, thought Karl, but he knew arguing wouldn't get him anywhere. "I can't do it today," he said, "Tiny's watching the intersection. With the minigun, you know. And the witch always goes out on Wednesday mornings, so it'll be our best chance. And, um, Mum said—"

"Fine," said Beth, "but we're coming to get you first thing tomorrow. Be ready."

They passed the rest of the day lolling about inside, away from the punishing heat. Karl couldn't settle. Too shaken by the skirmish with Tiny, too nervous about his task tomorrow. When he got home, his mum was waiting for him.

"Had an interesting call from Jock Farquharson today," she said. "Have you been throwing dead birds in his pool?"

"What? No!"

"Mmhmm. Not something that Beth Nguyen put you up to?"

"Mum, no! Why would we throw dead birds in his pool?"

"Well, someone's doing it. I didn't think it'd be you lot, and I told Jock that, but I had to ask. What were you doing in his yard?"

"I was – it was just a short-cut. I won't do it again, I promise!"

"Mmhmm. Your hands are filthy, go and wash up for dinner."

That night he tossed and turned, dreams filled with Barber Street boys, with murders of crows, and with the witch, tall and terrible and tattooed, russet-haired and cloaked in starlight. In the dream he tried to avoid her, tried to fill his lungs and hold it so she couldn't take his soul, but he could feel his breath caught, fleeing his body, stolen from him, leaving him gasping and breathless like he'd been tackled without forewarning.

As promised the Gilchrist Street army arrived at his place bright and early the next morning. Beth led them in the chorused good mornings to his mum; Karl tried to delay things as long as possible, but Beth and his mum were quickly conspiring to get the kids out of the house "before the day got too hot."

Far too soon they were standing on the purple carpet of jacaranda flowers on the nature strip before the gardener's place. It was quiet, still, and warming already. Bees buzzed lazily in the lavender and some hidden bird warbled away from the nectarine trees. In the jacaranda sat the crow, watching the proceedings as usual. It had no friendly greetings for Karl this morning.

Beth was watching him watching the house. "You'll be right, Karl," she said when he turned to look at her. "We'll be right out here, keeping watch. Her main car's not here, right? She'll be out somewhere. Just get inside, get something decent, and get back out."

"Leave your rifle," said Fish, "I'll look after it. Not much good against a gardener, I reckon."

"Just call her the witch!" squeaked Patio, rolling his eyes, but even he was more subdued in the shadow of the overgrown house.

Beth watched him, still. She'd taken off the aviators, her gaze level and clear. "You'll be right, Karl," she said again, quietly. "You'll be the one to save the Gilchrist Street army, won't you?"

He gulped. "Yes Beth."

"On your way then, soldier."

He slipped past the mailbox and into the garden. It was a riot of colour and blooms; the witch had a talent for keeping things colourful well past spring and into the dead heat of summer, and never seemed to be using water to keep the place fed. It was cool in here, cooler than it had any right to be in this summer heatwave, dappled light and deep shadows that hid all manner of imagined terrors. Karl steeled himself and crept down to the old ute that never seemed to move from the carport, felt around under the back wheel-arch.

When his fingers grasped the key, he wasn't sure whether he felt relieved or disappointed.

He stood, waved to the others out on the street, and stepped quietly up to the front door. The door was painted teal, peeling away in places. He pressed his ear to it but could hear nothing inside.

A deep breath. He unlocked the door and slipped inside.

The foyer was filled with more plants, dozens of ferns and cactuses and hanging things he couldn't identify. A circular mirror above a table, keys and coins scattered across it; on an old wicker chair sat a collection of hats. Nothing seemed particularly magical. He stepped into the next room.

He saw the artwork first, and blushed. More plants, a TV showing replays of the cricket on mute, a long green couch...and the witch, curled up with a cup of tea in hand.

"Good morning, Karl," she said, after a moment.

"Ah, um," said Karl.

She was wearing green corduroy overalls over a short-sleeved white t-shirt, and he could see all the tattoos of flowers and fish that covered her from wrist to shoulder. Sitting on a perch just behind her head was a huge black cockatoo, glaring at Karl out of one beady little eye.

"Urgh," gurgled Karl unhappily.

The witch uncurled her legs from beneath her and placed the mug on the low coffee table, covered with knick-knacks and bric-a-brac. "Can I help you with something?"

Karl looked at the ceiling. More hanging plants, and a skylight. "Your, um, your car..."

"It's getting serviced, darling. Did you need a ride somewhere?"

"No, um. We thought you, uh, you might be able to help us," said Karl, "with the Barber Street kids. And their, you know, their new arsenal."

The witch picked up a little tube of some mysterious unguent or salve, and Karl felt his hopes raise. Then she uncapped it, and he realised it was only hand cream, like his mum used. The witch said, "These are your mates that you're playing the wargames with, is it?" Karl nodded. "And they've got new toys, hmm? Unusual ones?"

"They've got a flame-thrower! And a minigun!" said Karl. The words started tumbling out now, as if he'd smashed the piñata and all the lollies were dribbling through the hole. "Not like real ones, they still shoot pellets or berries or whatever. I mean, the flame-thrower seemed pretty real. But they don't really seem to leave Barber Street or the alleyway with any of them!"

The witch grinned at him but said nothing.

"And, we thought maybe you might have something magic we could use to, you know, get them back, a bit. They trapped Beth and Patio in Morely's shed!"

"Well, we can't be having that, can we?" The witch picked up the mug again, cradling it in both hands as if the morning was cold. "I think I know what's happened, Karl, and I think I can help. But I'll need something from you in return."

Here it was, Karl thought. He was going to have his soul stolen in return for some dumb magic beans or something. He thought of Beth and her bravery, of Patio's chest wound and Fish's head injury. They had to do something.

"Okay," he said with only the barest tremor in his voice. "What do you want?"

"I need some help in the garden, actually," said the witch. "The four of you on summer holidays should make light work of a bit of pruning and weeding, hmm?"

The relief in Karl's chest was palpable. "Yeah! Yeah, of course."

She grinned again, that same smile. It was somehow both open and devious, like you were being let in on an inside joke, and it made him a little less afraid of her. The cockatoo squawked loudly.

"Hush," said the witch to the bird, and then to Karl, "It's a deal. One of my little friends got out the other day," she gestured vaguely around the room, "and I suspect they've been trapped in Jock Farquharson's pool. Lots of salt in that pool, you see, but I've heard Jock complaining these last few nights. If the kids have been offering things to the creature in the pool, that'd explain the provenance of these weapons. Though in my experience the weapons of the other realm are usually a bit nastier."

Karl absorbed this information. "They've been throwing dead birds in there," he said after a moment. "Mr Farquharson called Mum to accuse me of doing it, but I never!"

"Of course not," said the witch. "And I recommend you don't. For one thing, Jock's not likely to forget, and of course the creature only gets greedier. My little friend is trapped and will want to escape; granting half-formed wishes from playful tots is not their idea of a good time, I can assure you. Easiest solution will be to go and pluck them out." She saw Karl's apprehensive glance. "Use a bucket! Fill it with something tasty and my friend will wander straight in. Then bring them back to me, job done."

"Okay," said Karl. "Um, but what about the weapons they already have?"

The witch smiled again, unsettlingly wide. "Oh, leave that part to me. And Karl?" He nodded, eyes wide. "Put the keys back when you head out, won't you darling?"

Outside, the others were leaning casually against the fence, keeping a practised eye on the other side of the intersection. Fish spotted him first. "What'd you get, Karl? How are we going to win this?"

"She said to use a bucket," said Karl.

"She said?" asked Beth immediately. "You spoke to her?"

"What good is a fucking bucket?" said Fish. "You dumb fuck Karl, you were supposed to find a weapon!"

Karl ignored Fish, which was usually the best response. "She said fill a bucket with tasty things and take it to Farquharson's pool. There's a – there's something living in there, and the Barber Street kids are feeding it, and it's giving them the weapons in return. And she said if we did that, she'd take care of the Barber Street kids' weapons. And we have to do some gardening for her."

Patio looked aghast. "Forced labour! I'm not doing, like, chores for some dumb stoner."

"You will," said Beth. "This all makes sense. When you were in the pool, Patio, didn't you feel it? A hunger." Patio nodded reluctantly. Beth continued, "We haven't got any other plans. So."

The four of them looked at one another. "I have a bucket we can use," said Fish.

"And I can raid Mum's chocolate stash," said Karl.

"Good idea. Everyone find something tasty you've been saving, and we'll meet back at base. Steer clear of any of the usual battlegrounds."

Half an hour later the Gilchrist Street army made their approach to Farquharson's place. Patio was on point and was the first to spot the Barbers down the alleyway. "Scatter!" he squeaked. The pellets raised a curtain of ochre dust from the alley floor. Karl threw himself sideways behind an old wheelie bin. He could hear Beth yelling, exhorting them to fire back. He risked a look over the bin. Through the dust he glimpsed Tiny, minigun whirring as it spat pellets everywhere. Beside Tiny, Jackson fired the huge bazooka with a solid whump. Fish smashed into the bin beside Karl.

"Still got the bucket?" he yelled. Karl nodded. "Get over the wall. I'm going to try and circle round to the other end of the alleyway. Patio and Beth'll distract 'em here. You do some backyard jumping and stay out of sight!" Fish cupped his hands and braced his back against the cinder-block wall. "Come on! I'll boost you."

"Karl," called the crow, somewhere nearby. Karl pressed his foot into Fish's hands and scrambled to the top of the wall. The minigun stopped. He risked a look down the alleyway from his momentary vantage point.

At the Barber Street end of the alleyway, Tiny and the other kids had stood to the sides. Making room, Karl could see now. Into their midst stepped a giant.

Taller even than Tiny, a complex structure of PVC pipes and duct tape formed a giant exoskeleton around Rob 'Daylight' Berry, the leader of the Barber Street goons. The madcap construction took another step, raising more dust. The creature's arms were two huge PVC cannons, aimed squarely at the Gilchrist Street army. Through the swirling dirt Karl could see Daylight's face in sharp focus, smirking in triumph.

Then a small pellet hit Daylight right between his stupid beady little eyes. "BETH!" roared the furious child in the DIY mech.

"Karl!" cawed the crow, and Karl slid off the wall and into the backyard just as the alleyway erupted.

Karl scrambled for the fence between the yards, dropped the bucket over and followed as elegantly as he could. On the other side a couple of kids had abandoned a cricket match and were peering over the wall at the insanity in the alleyway. He grabbed the bucket, checked it hadn't spilled any of the cargo, and snuck past unnoticed.

One yard to go. This one a desolate expanse of concrete, no shade to speak of. He could just about see the heat rising from it. Nothing for it but to race.

He crossed the yard in what felt like three huge bounds and scrambled over the fence. Farquharson's place. No sign of the man. Pool right there. Easy as pie.

Too easy. Tiny was standing beside the alley wall. Surely the kid wasn't tall enough to peer over, even at his height? "Fuck off, Karly," said the giant, and the minigun set to work. Karl felt the sting again, welts across his chest and side, little blooms of heat and pain. He stumbled forwards and fell into Farquharson's pool.

The water felt cool, but the chlorine hit the back of his nostrils like an artillery shell. He tried to surface.

Karl, something said.

He spun around, eyes stinging, starting. At the bottom of the pool, under the water, sat a bedraggled little crow. It looked at him with a black and glinting gaze. Something like ink bled from it into the water. Karl, it said again. Pellets spun through the water around him. He swam down, closer to the crow, bucket dragging behind him. Karl.

His breath burned in his chest. He held out the bucket, filled with chocolates and mulberries and all the food treasures an eleven-year-old can hoard. The little bird dragged itself into the bucket, and Karl felt a strong hand grab him around the neck and haul him from the water.

He found himself looking up into the barred moustache of a furious Mr Farquharson.

A week later, when his mum had finally lifted his life sentence and he could return to the street, he took the little crow in its little bucket home back to the witch.

"Hello, my little friend," she cooed at him, "let's get you dried out. Teach you to go wandering where you're not wanted!"

"Is it...are they talking to me?" asked Karl. "When they call out, it sounds like my name." He blushed, but he had to know.

"Oh, probably. Who knows what crows do? Not all of them are as clever, or as foolish, as my little friend here, and they certainly don't all grant wishes or sit at the bottoms of pools. Only especially foolish ones, hey mate?" she asked the crow, who somehow contrived to look sheepish. "I suspect some of his mates around here have pegged you as someone who might be good to make friends with. Not everyone pays much attention to the desires of birds."

Karl mulled over this for a while. "Beth said that the Barber Street boys' toys all fell apart when we came out of the pool. That was you, wasn't it? Can you teach me how to do the magic?"

The witch grinned. "You and your mates owe me a summer of gardening yet, Karl."

Once he left the witch's place, Karl headed back to the base in the Parson's backyard. The others were waiting for him, and an endless summer of victory stretched ahead. The weight of the tiny magic wand the crow had helped him construct during his week-long grounding was a promise, tucked into his waistband and hidden by his shirt.

A NIGHT IN THE VALLEY, BY CHRIS LEGO
CHAPTER – LISMORE, NSW

Warren looked at Alex then back at the worn-out key in his hand. He thought about Alex's quiet proposal as the intoxicants and stimulants of the last few hours swarmed lazily through his bloodstream. The babble of the house party swam around him and he was suddenly aware of how many people were in the kitchen and how warm it was.

"Maybe" he said and was suddenly aware of how quietly he'd said it and how dry his mouth was. Guitars blared on the sound system in the other room on mismatched speakers that were straining to keep up with the volume. Distorted distortion.

He wondered if key parties were always this loud and raucous or if was just a feature of partying in the Central West, in a medium sized town near Orange. Or maybe it was a product of the times. Strange times.

He sipped his wine out of the chipped mug and looked at Alex and the curve of her jawline in the sweaty greasy fluoro light of the kitchen. He smiled, feeling how unsure his smile was and said 'Maybe' again, feeling how much he had to force the smile and the word out. He needed to get his shit together.

Alex caught his eyes and returned his smile. 'Lets go outside' she said and the two of then slipped outside the back door, pausing a bit as the light in the doorway was replaced by a more ambient glow of the backyard, with people scattered around a fire and a few lanterns among the scruffy garden.

Their eyes readjusted as there was a few popping sounds from the back of the yard. Warren suddenly felt unsure about all of this, the whole night in fact. He supposed it was better than another night reading by candlelight in the back of his van all by himself, but it was hard to not feel totally alone, even in a crowded party where everyone seemed to be on at least nodding terms with each other. Intoxicants can only take you so far. Alex's hand brushed his as they stood at the edge of the fire light, then there were more popping sounds. Warren suddenly realised that they sounded like the sound of a .22 rifle, the explosive nature of them dulled by the drunken salad of noise from the party.

The little wooden house thudded and shook with the bass from the stereo and the sound of dozens of conversations, some whispered and some yelled. He looked up the side of the house to the tangle of vehicles at the front of the house, past the overgrown carpet of grass and the inevitable junk that a house of 20 somethings seemed to gather, spilling out from under the house. Two figures embraced each other in the edge of the bamboo that ran along the side fence and Warren turned back quickly towards the fire.

Looking back, he could see more people in uncertain light up the end of the yard, their outlines against a lopsided corrugated iron fence.

Alex took Warren's wine out of this unsuspecting hand and said something quietly. Warren leaned in and said 'sorry'? as Alex smiled at his closeness. Warren felt way out of his depth. Alex seemed to read his mind and their smile lingered as she sipped Warrens wine. 'I said maybe we should have some fun up the back with Charlie and Felix?'.

Warren wondered what kind of fun had to happen at this party up the back of the yard by candlelight when there were plates of sticky trucker speed going around in a fog of dope smoke in the lounge room and everyone's keys in a fish-bowl on the coffee table. And who the fuck were Charlie and Felix?

He shook himself slightly as he helplessly nodded at Alex, reminding himself that he was out here to do new things and have adventures, even by accident. That is why he drove away from the wary stale sameness of suburban Sydney a few months ago.

That popping sound again.

They meandered up the long yard on a path beaten into the unbowed grass, past a half-hearted veggie garden, the tomatoes looking like neglected camouflage for the two weed plants in the middle of it all. The figures up the back swam into soft focus. Felix was arranging an array of cheap looking plaster figures from a Christmas nativity scene on a small set of wooden shelves, his jaw clenched in a grin and his eyes shining, hair spilling out from under a trucker cap that proclaimed that he'd been at the Orange Christian Youth Camp of 1978. If he'd been there in any capacity apart from being escorted off the property, Warren would have been surprised.

Charlie was casually holding the rifle and saw Warrens expression. "Don't worry Captain" he boomed. "It's just an air rifle, mostly I use it to shoot rats at the tip. The wood behind the shelves will catch any stray pellets."

Warren had the thought that having sex with Alex suddenly seemed a lot better option than shooting figurines of the three wise men with these trashed guys. His libido stirred for the first time in ages and he was suddenly aware of Alex's car key in his jeans pocket. He wondered where his car key was, if it was still in a tangle with the others in a fish-bowl that had never been used for anything else than pairing people off in the lounge-room or if someone had his in their pocket and had been checking him out in the swarm of people inside.

He shook his head again and looked over at Alex, who seemed transfixed by Felix arranging the statues carefully as if they weren't about to get shot at by Charlie who was loading the rifle, fishing for pellets inside his top pocket absentmindedly.

"I don't know about this" Warren suddenly said. "I'm not really a gun kinda guy."

Charlie looked up briefly, looked at the two of them and then snapped the rifle shut with a shrug and a smile. "That's cool man" he said in a voice that seemed tailor made to heckle a crowd. 'Just chill and watch'. He hoisted the rifle to his shoulder as Felix casually stood back against the fence.

The body of a plaster sheep the size of a beer can suddenly exploded into shards and its head spun and dropped to the shelf staring forward. Like a hunter with bloodshot eyes he reloaded in a few seconds and the figure of Joseph shattered into pieces.

Felix whooped and Warren stepped backwards as Alex caught his hand. "It's cool, Charlie is a crack shot."

Warren wasn't sure about that, they were only a few metres away but he guessed that the warmth of Alex's hand was more of a pressing issue right now. And it was only an air rifle.

It had been a long few months in his van and he was suddenly aware of Alex's eyes on him. He half turned and looked at Alex who was even closer to him. Felix was casually observing them as he leant against the fence sipping a beer, unconcerned about standing a few metres away from the targets of Charlie's rifle.

He smiled and nodded at Warren, without the smile reaching his eyes.

He seemed to smile his approval.

Charlie looked from the targets to Warren and Alex standing there holding hands. Time seemed to stop and Charlie shrugged and raised the air rifle again to his shoulder. Plaster shattered and the music in the house was turned up even more. The sound of warring conversations and laughter swelled. Alex squeezed his hand. Warren felt himself blushing and he took a step backwards unconsciously away from the guys with the rifle, casually shooting at statues like apocalyptic carnies.

Alex misread his caution and stepped back with him, their hips touching now. 'What are we doing back here if you're scared of guns?'.

Warren thought that was fair question. The house had just seemed too intense, but back here was a different kind of intense. In between the watchful eyes of Charlie and Felix and Alex's hip against his he felt a bit trapped in this corner of the yard despite his growing libido which felt like coming out of a slumber.

He didn't have much choice though.

He glanced to the side and looked at the row of burnt out houses.

Empty windows like eye sockets looked back.

The house was an island of noise and light in a sea of quietness and the edge of the darkness felt like an ominous cloak all of a sudden. He wondered how many eyes were watching the house.

He suddenly realised that Charlie and Felix were there to seal off people jumping the back fence. When he'd driven into the valley and been stopped by the Blacklists he'd realised that he couldn't leave easily now but he didn't realise they had a breeding program, as dressed up as it was with wine and booze and the trappings of a 1970s key party.

They had a bigger plan than a captive workforce and making substandard wine it seems.

The thing was that the valley was sealed off with tyre spikes over the roads and quietly aggressive Blacklists with a variety of weapons who reeked of amphetamines and control despite their facade of friendliness. The monopoly of violence was theirs.

Warren looked over at Alex, resigned to what had to happen next. All the alcohol in his system didn't feel like enough all of a sudden, as cute as Alex was, even after the slow collapse of everything a few years ago. Many things had disappeared, including choice in this particular pocket of the world in what used to be known as New South Wales.

They were a few of those that were left, the gang had sealed them in the valley deftly after they had drifted in looking for safety and food and kept them as a workforce making wine from stolen vineyards, and kept hooked on a constant and free supply of food and speed pills that seemed to be made in the old church in the middle of town. Warren had never seen a church with a razor wire fence around it before he landed in this town.

It seemed like a place of new precedents, its original name had even been scrubbed from the physical fibre of the town. The gang just referred to it as the Base, and they were mindful of telling people how good they had it here with a weekly food and wine allowance and freedom after work hours to do what they wanted. 'The alternatives outside are much worse, especially without a hand' he'd been told as they looted his battered van before driving it and him into town They made him ride in the back, sweating and thinking he was going to throw up, even while his favourite Fugazi cassette played in his ancient tape deck.

He supposed they were protected and safe. Until they wanted to leave, and bought it up with any of their minders, the members of the gang that were slightly bigger than the others who had the crossed-out circle tattooed on the back of their hands.

It'd been two years now and he had only caught a glimpse of the supposed leader of the gang who ruled the valley. He guessed that being notorious and mysterious was more effective than being famous. It was easier to instill fear about an unknown ruler than a human you could put a face to. It had worked for organised religion for a long time.

He supposed that life here was OK, maybe they were right; it could be a lot worse, even as a shy fellow who still lived in his van down by the river. It hadn't run in a long time, but they made people hang onto their car keys for the promise of the next tanker of fuel. The petrol never reached the workers of the valley though. The Blacklists didn't want a mobile population of course. A captive workforce kept just hungry enough and addicted enough was much easier to control.

Along with regular bread and circus type events such as tonight's effort.

Unlimited wine couldn't disguise the threat of a beating if they didn't fuck in one of the vans out the front of the house, grass long around their wheels and a mattress in every one. They had ceased to be vehicles and become conception cabins in the last few months. A roster of essential attendees were told when they had to come to this party house.

He wondered if Alex was as conscious as him in that moment about their lack of options.

He glanced back towards Charlie, noticing the tattooed hand casually still on the rifle. There hadn't been any popping sounds or shattering plaster in a while when he had been lost in his thoughts.

Charlie nodded at him as he felt Alex's hand tighten on his, his missing fingers suddenly noticeable to him even after almost three years.

"Go on then" he growled, his loud voice suddenly clear with threat. The barrel was suddenly pointed at his legs. 'Number three is free. You'd better do it.'

Warren and Alex turned and walked down the side of the house towards the stripped vans in a sea of grass. He caught sight of her resigned face in the half darkness, slightly gaunt.

He wondered if it really was Saturday night as they climbed into the van, lit by a rough candle that was possibly made from human fat. The days had stopped having names and he wondered if this was what it felt like to be farmed as the slid the rusty door shut.

HIGHLY COMMENDED

THE DOLL, BY VINCE G. AUGUST
CHAPTER –PORT MACQUARIE, NSW

"Mmmm?"

He'd vagued out and missed what Ned had said. A sudden degree of urgency in her voice brought him back, but it was too late. He had no thread at which to grasp. "What were you saying?"

Hamish continued watching the barista over his flat white. She looked the goods but he feared the coffee would be shit. The mobile felt warmer against his ear than the cup to his lips. Not good.

"I was saying make sure you get the doll."

It was all Hamish could do not to sigh. Wincing silently at the word "doll", he took a sip, which had the unfortunate effect of making him wince audibly.

"Don't start in on me again," Ned warned. "I don't care what it's called, you know what I mean. And you know that's what Jamie calls it, so you need to get used to it."

"Yeah, righto!" Hamish protested. "That wasn't at you... This coffee's awful."

"My shallowest sympathies, darling. If that's the worst of your problems, you're having a better morning than I am. Jamie's miserable. I think it's another ear infection, and the party's tomorrow." Ned slowed down, which was a thing she did when she wanted Hamish to know she was pissed off. "Get. The. Doll."

Hamish knew when to cut and run.

"I know it's his birthday. I'll get it."

He ended the call before it could get worse. Contemplating the coffee, Hamish thought better of it, sighed and returned his attention to the barista.

"You just can't trust people these days," he muttered. Pocketing the mobile and taking his bag, he hit the street.

***

The meeting had been guano. Hamish's presence had not been required. He'd suspected as much when his micro-managing, macro-arsed supervisor had tasked him with going. Knowing he would not be called on for input, Hamish had let his mind wander. If one more dickhead prattled on about "gaining traction", "moving forward" or "value adding", he didn't want to hear them.

Doll! For fuck's sake.

Neridah had been a safe bet. It wasn't that he'd settled. It was more that the string of girlfriends that had preceded her were, in different ways and directions, off the fucking chain. The surfing community was tight knit, locally speaking. There were few randoms, so things were fairly predictable. Go national, though, and it seemed you couldn't turn around without humping into a Betty crazier than the last.

Wave led on to wave and the novelty wore off after a few years. Fluctuating results and generally paltry prize-money meant scorn-worthy income, and the transient lifestyle became less Endless Summer and more endless bummer. Hamish was over it, so he braced himself for the mandatory shit he would cop from the diehards and went corporate. Taking a job repping for one of the tour's major sponsors, he left 420 behind for cocaine, suddenly everywhere and suddenly affordable. The future had never featured before, but experiencing what he had to assume was a maturation spurt, Hamish felt himself in it. He met Neridah while spruiking the company's product and not long after they were partying, albeit with a restraint that was, to Hamish, vexing and intriguing in equal measure.

"Keep going. You're not boring me," joked the old boiler to Hamish's right as she rose and moved to the drip-filtered coffee at the front of the meeting room. She poured herself a cup and sneaked a look at her male colleague who had been talking up the company's customers, assuring the room that brand loyalty wasn't dead and vigorous marketing would see off the Amazon effect. Hamish watched discreetly as the coveted prattled on, ignoring his admirer and, it seemed, all present.

No one cares, you clueless clown. Hamish pushed back in his chair and stretched his neck, tilting his head left and right, forwards and backwards. He continued for as long as he dared, mindful that it wouldn't do to look uninterested, and eventually transitioned from neck to legs by getting up for a coffee himself. Hamish had had a bump after showering, but felt he'd need another if he was going to survive this meeting. The coffee smelt good, at least, and the steam issuing from the stream Hamish poured into an off-white cup promised it would be hot.

That barista. Stripper hair, snake bites and fuck-you if you-don't like-it eyes. Hamish wondered how much energy people could have left over after investing so much in their look. Still, something hinted at untapped reserves behind the black apron. Something inviting. Inviting without the invitation.

"We just need a critical mass of retailers to stock this line and it's a winner," asserted a shirt across the table.

Watch it cunt, thought Hamish, implying agreement with an almost pensive nod while simultaneously taking a sip of water to ensure that's where it ended. Pursing his lips to hold the tepid liquid around his teeth, he doubled down on the move, and spun his pen around his thumb and across the back of his hand before catching it and repeating the process several times. It was a practised technique at distraction. Anyone who might have expected him to weigh in was now certain he would not and, Hamish liked to think, just a little intimidated by the trick.

Intriguing. That had been what it was. What Neridah was. Exuding both a warm charm and cool logic in her dealings with clients (and eminently more qualified than Hamish), she impressed her superiors and advancement followed. Rocking a gym-honed body and chic lodgings in a desirable postcode, it was no surprise she impressed Hamish. It was a surprise when pregnancy soon followed. At the time there had been rumours of an offer. State manager. Neridah said nothing, so neither did Hamish. He adopted a policy of general agreement with whatever Neridah said, supposing that this was what it meant to be a supportive partner. She suggested the pregnancy be allowed to run its natural course and offered Hamish a choice: in or out. Showing a degree of common sense often lacking only months earlier, he'd bitten down on the temptation to note that it was in and out that had led them to this juncture and hugged Neridah his in-ness.

The coffee had cooled quickly and Hamish drained the last of it just as a new presenter called for "comments slash questions". A cold coffee kind of day, he thought.

Jamie had meant a halt to the advancement, but Neridah had retained her position. Although still a managerial force with which to be reckoned, her career had plateaued across the three years she had added "mother" to her dot-point list of roles and responsibilities. Not that Hamish would every say the word "plateaued" aloud in her presence. I might not have a uni degree, but a man's not a fucking idiot, he mused.

***

"Thanks for sitting in, mate."

It was the critical mass shirt.

"No worries. Not sure I was really needed, though," Hamish replied, hopeful he had left no room for follow ups.

The elevator was always the worst. Hamish had once faked towards the toilets and taken the stairs down to avoid this type of pointless nicety. When he reached the ground floor a sign had warned him an alarm would sound if the door before him was opened. When he opened the door, the alarm sounded. He hadn't expected that and, paralysed by indecision, been embarrassed when a security guard unlikely to do the hundred metres in under a minute had found him still holding the door open, a foot each side of the threshold, torn between advancing despite the din or beating a hasty retreat back up the stairs.

"Like to celebrate our freedom with a drink?" the shirt asked with a jokey smile.

"Nah, sorry. I've gotta go shopping for my son's birthday. He's three tomorrow and if I don't get it sorted..." What other situation-appropriate details could he proffer to dissuade debate or counter-offer? Hamish was considering moving into situation-inappropriate territory when the elevator settled to a rest and the doors opened, presenting him with his escape. "I've really gotta go. It was nice to meet you though."

Clean away, thought Hamish as he strode through the foyer and out onto the footpath.

***

The shopping centre was the generic confusion of brand name outlets, shambolic food courts and intensely bright lighting. People hurried this way and that, some speaking at elevated volume and often in languages Hamish couldn't being to guess at. Groups of middle-aged women, clad head to toe in designer active wear, sat at tables and on benches sipping concoctions outrageous in size, colour and price. Younger women pushed prams and strollers cow plough-like ahead of their locomotive determination not to expose their envy. Men were fewer in number, generally solitary, and - ponderous maintenance staff aside - more mysterious in purpose. What pressing need brought you here? wondered Hamish, reasoning they couldn't all have sons turning three tomorrow. Accepting the enigma would have to remain beyond his comprehension, he walked onwards until he found himself in front of his pre-programed destination. A deep breath later and he was inside.

Hamish's eyes scanned upwards looking, it appeared, for divine guidance. He found it in the form of a ceiling-suspended 'toys and games' sign, and pressed on into the bowels of the store. His shortest-path-between-two-points-is-a-straight-line approach soon proved folly, however, and he found himself unwillingly wending his way through aisles bordered by racks upon racks of merchandise he doggedly ignored. Repeated right angle turns left and right disorientated him to such a degree he became increasingly uncertain as to just how much progress he had made towards his destination. Like a narrow ravine's unforgiving walls, the racks cut down Hamish's angles, affording him views of little more than the ceiling directly overhead. Exasperated, he was halfway through a 360 degree bearing check when rescue appeared in the form of a store worker.

Young and carrying a hand-held inventory booper, she looked almost as surprised as Hamish felt delivered from some perverse new circle of hell.

"Can I help you, sir?"

"Yes," Hamish started to smile his relief, but faltered as his immediate surroundings came into focus "I mean, no... Not here."

He was in the women's underwear section. Hamish blinked. The women's plus size underwear section. Feeling blood rush to his ears and cheeks, he felt he had cast himself off from the edge of the known world a minute earlier and now found himself capsised in an ocean of multi-coloured monsters, desperately clinging to the punctured life raft of his rapidly deflating dignity.

"I'm looking for a toy!" he blurted.

Her eyes flicked left and almost, thought Hamish in panic, rolled upwards. Her focus re-centring, but head tilting slightly, she offered him salvation.

"The toy department?"

"Yeah... yes," Hamish stammered.

"It's this way."

Following her, Hamish breathed deeply to regain some composure. As she led him out of his torture, he took in the form of his liberator as though actually seeing her for the first time. She was neither short nor tall and, imagining his way through the bland store uniform, Hamish saw a body made for surfing. Powerful legs and tight glutes supported a strong core, while lithe arms, slender neck and a proportionally narrow head suggested grace and balance. Little machine, Hamish smiled at his silent compliment.

"Here we are. Was there something in particular you were looking for?"

She had stopped and turned quickly, and Hamish wondered if it was a deliberate action to catch him perving – which, if so, he feared had succeeded – or natural confidence in her navigation.

"Uh, yeah. A Spiderman plush toy. It's for my..." Hamish hesitated for a moment that felt like a minute "my nephew."

Her eyes were black and they considered Hamish for an equally indefinable period.

"Cool," she said evenly "Down here."

She's gorgeous, Hamish realised as she turned away from him again. He followed quickly, not wanting to lose her. As he pursued her gently bobbing body, though, a frown crossed his brow. He furiously sought to justify his lie, but abandoned all hope when his efforts netted only the truth. The girl, for Hamish guessed her age at not yet twenty, was something he wanted. Something he missed.

"There's different sizes. Other characters, too," she gestured at the end of another aisle.

Hamish looked and saw what he had been sent to find.

"They say these are the new dolls. Like, not just a trend," Elizabeth – Hamish had been clocking her nametag and the slight but definite curve on which it rested – offered with undetected hope.

"That's what my par... parents are calling it," Hamish had spoken too quickly, too loudly and scrambled to regroup his thoughts. "Seems wrong..." he petered out.

"Why?"

"I dunno," he attempted ambivalence "I just think these are more your garden variety stuffed toy. Someone says 'doll' and you immediately think of Barbie... Cabbage Patch... that kind of thing."

"Do I?" The black eyes seemed to look through Hamish and he had the unsettling sensation that he was being assessed against criteria he would not meet, far less understand. Floundering, he abruptly changed tact in the hope the girl would follow him into what he hoped were safer waters.

"Do you surf?" he asked.

"Surf?" Her tone was flat and Hamish couldn't read her face. He thought he saw one eyebrow arch upward minutely, but it might have been that the other had lowered itself momentarily, dragged downwards by the possibly suspicious eye beneath. This is hopeless, he cursed himself before rallying for one final effort. He smiled gamely.

"Yeah, surf! You know... boards, waves, sand in your shorts and whatnot?"

"No," the girl laughed and paused, seeming to weigh something in her mind before continuing. "I'm a volley-baller." She saw Hamish's confusion. The same confusion she always had to allay in those unfamiliar with the game. "I play libero. In the back-court. No net for me."

"Libero in the back-court," Hamish played with the words. "Sounds exotic. And intriguing..."

A silence slid in from the side and nudged its way between them. Hamish held her gaze and she his, but as the silence refused to slide on past them he felt it was becoming more awkward for him than for the girl. He picked up a Spiderman, tossed it and caught it.

"Anyway," he smiled widely to conceal his uncertainty. "You've fixed me up big time here. Wish I could return the favour..." Hamish wanted to let his words hang, but the girl spoke immediately and he felt the momentum of the moment shift in a direction he didn't like.

"What's your nephew's name?"

"My nephew?" he felt himself gaping gormlessly.

"Your nephew. That's not for you, right?" she nodded at the Spiderman.

"Oh, shit... nah. It's for my nephew for sure... Hamish."

"Okay. For Hamish it is, then. I'm Elizabeth," she did a game-show hostess hand flourish in front of her nametag "You are?"

The momentum had definitely shifted and the speed of parlay had suddenly increased, making Hamish unsure what treachery lay beneath the wake of his spontaneous lies.

"Jamie. I'm Jamie," he laughed. "Or James, if you want," he revised, clearly trying to make the name more palatable to his own tongue.

"I think Jamie's better." Elizabeth grinned, but with what looked to Hamish grim dissatisfaction more than good humour. He sensed he wasn't going to reel this one in. It was time to cut and run.

"Anyway, thanks again." Hamish did his own elaborate hand flourish in front of the Spiderman. "I'd better not keep you."

Elizabeth laughed at the gesture and held her smile.

"Okay, then." Her eyes told Hamish that the moment needn't end and he felt himself further at sea again.

"Look," he tried to mirror her smile. "I'm flying back to Melbourne tomorrow. You can have this if you want it. I'm just down the road..."

He took his room key from his pocket and offered it to Elizabeth, who looked at it benignly, but made no move to accept it. Hamish grimaced in embarrassment. Or was it the shame? He couldn't say. He pocketed the key and turned to escape his failure.

"Wait. I get off at three."

Hamish turned to see Elizabeth's open hand extended. Her face impassive and body motionless, she looked like a statue memorialising some long ago expeditionary who, with objective determined and course decided, was certain victory lay waiting ahead. Wordlessly, he handed her the key, paused, thinking better of it, and then turned again. He left without looking back.

***

Outside the shopping centre, the world rotated on its axis. Hamish felt himself being spun along with it, as though he was no longer afforded unconscious immunity to its alarming speed. As though it had sped up suddenly and he was the only one who noticed. The traffic and construction noise, effectively muted inside the centre, resumed with vengeance once he exited its artificial atmosphere. He passed a ramp descending to a dimly lit loading dock and screwed up his nose at the warm draught it emitted. Peering into its gloomy depths, Hamish felt queasy at the sight of people there, toiling among a stench he could only liken to rotten vegetables mopped up with oily rags. Hurrying on, he looked away from a beggar collapsed in on himself behind a handwritten sign that read "HOMELESS" and a filthy beanie containing depressingly few coins. Across the street he saw a row of empty storefronts, with a wholesale butchery, a discount store and an adult shop the only signs of endeavor, and Hamish wondered if it was centre management's proclivities or exorbitant rent that kept them out here in this awful otherworld.

He was relieved to reach the frosted-glass front of his hotel.

With cold glass in hand, Hamish took a seat in the street level bar that shared the premises. He placed his son's present, safe inside a glossy white plastic bag, on the table in front of him and drank greedily.

"Fuck me," he whispered, shaking his head slightly and placing his drink on the table. Looking into its carbonated nebula, Hamish sought to slow down. To find a familiar point of reference onto which he might grasp and recalibrate – no - re-anchor his existence. The sweeping second hand of an otherwise minimalistic clock on the wall opposite him caught Hamish's attention and he followed its arc until it passed twelve. All else was ablur and abuzz, but one thing was certain.

It was three o'clock.

Hamish's mind crunched numbers. The time it would take for a store worker to tie up any loose ends, sign off (or whatever they did), gather a bag if they had to and farewell any co-workers who might care they were leaving. Time added to allow for error, he figured half an hour. Three-thirty. If Elizabeth didn't show by then she wouldn't show at all. He would wait until four to be certain, then tell reception he had lost the key and deal with the consequences. No drama.

The ensuing thirty minutes, or thirty-one to be precise, were anything but no drama. They were thirty-one minutes of torturous rehearsal and rewrites. Hamish wasn't relieved when he saw Elizabeth enter the foyer carrying a plastic bag of her own and head straight to the elevators. Not relieved. Not jubilant. Not... What was he? Not sure he would like the answer, he considered other questions. Should he go forward? That was the way his afternoon had pushed him, yet should he back out? He couldn't. She was in his room. Now. There was no backing out. Nor was there any sliding left or right. He needed that room, company or no.

***

What the fuck is with elevator music?, thought Hamish as the doors parted and he bumped past them into the hallway, the plastic bag compressed between man and metal. A dozen steps and he was outside his room. The "Do not disturb" door hanger was between bolt and receiver. Hamish pushed the door and it dropped to the floor in silence.

It was silent inside, too, and dark. Torn by emotions from every direction a compass might point, Hamish inched forward, leaning into the door to prevent it swinging closed. From his position just inside the standard kitchenette to the right, bathroom to the left hall, he could see a figure prone, horizontal and motionless, on the bed. It appeared weightless, floating on the soft duvet rather than sinking into to its luxurious depths. Something was wrong. The lines, the abrupt curves, cast curious half-shadows thrown by the obligatory clock-radio and the hall lights peeking around Hamish's hesitant silhouette. Using his free hand, he felt for but couldn't find the switch cluster inside the door. Wrestling his phone from his pocket, Hamish hit the torch.

The phone rang.

The garishly circular mouth a silently screamed "O!"

Shocking orifices.

"Hello."

"Hey! It's me."

Impossibly improportionate breasts.

"Oh... hey..." It was the best he could muster confronted by the perverse balloon in front of him.

"Did you get the doll?"

Glossy plastic reflected the torch's light onto Hamish's startled face as the realisation he had been outplayed struck hard.

"Hamish?"

"... Uh... Yeah?"

A razor-thin seam circumnavigated the body horizontally.

"Did you get it? The doll?"

"Uh, yeah... Yeah, I got the doll."

The door clicked shut.

THE SMALL WOODEN BOX, BY ROB JENNINGS
CHAPTER – KINGSTON, TAS

'OK, here it is.' Higgo very gently laid a small wooden box with a hinged lid in the centre of the round table. Right in the middle, between all 5 of them.

Gaz opened the lid without picking the box up.

Inside, on a bed of crumpled red velvet, was a small brass key.

Nine eyes darted around the room looking hopefully for someone else to say or do something, desperately trying to present an expression that conveyed enough understanding so as not to appear ignorant, but not so much as to be expected to take the initiative. One eye simply rested lazily behind its patch, minding its own business.

'It's a key.'

Once Dusty said this, everyone relaxed a little. It was, quite obviously, a key. They were all thinking "it's a key" but clearly no one wanted to say "it's a key". It would be a ball-tearingly stupid thing to say in this circumstance. There's a reason they called this kind of statement "doing a Dusty".

Higgo smiled nervously. 'Huh. Yeah, I guess it is.'

Gaz turned to Higgo. 'Wait, are you saying you didn't know it was a key?'

'Well. Yes. But, well. No. I mean they guy said it would unlock the answer to all our problems. I'll admit I didn't expect it to be an actual key. But I gotta hand it to the guy, it's definitely a key.'

Gaz decided that Higgo had definitely taken on the role of the idiot in this particular conversation, and so was no longer worried about asking obvious questions. 'A key to what, exactly?'

'Ah, well that's the question, isn't it?' Higgo smiled waggishly as he said this. Against all reason, he seemed to be enjoying himself which only fuelled Gaz's indignation.

'Believe me, Higgo, it's only the first of many, MANY, questions. But let's not get too far ahead of ourselves. What is this a key to, exactly?'

Dusty decided this was a great time to weigh in again. 'I'm guessing some kind of lock.'

'Another brilliant observation! Is it, Higgo? Is it indeed a key to some kind of lock?'

'Or it could be a locker. Or a door!' Dusty was on a roll this afternoon.

Franco was scratching his chin. He did this to appear thoughtful, and came across exactly like someone who was trying to appear thoughtful. 'For those things, a locker or a door, to need keys, though, they'd need a lock. Like you can't have a key that opens a door, unless that door has a lock. So the key would still be a key to a lock. Just a lock IN a door, or a lock IN a locker.' Franco said this, having come to the conclusion that he could say almost anything now and position himself nicely between the hole that Higgo was rapidly digging himself into and the building wrath of Gaz. If he had heard the story of Icarus, and had enough general intelligence to apply his knowledge of that story to his current situation, he might have looked at himself as choosing a flight-path between Higgo's ocean and Gaz's sun and felt very, very, smug about being smarter than some dead Greek guy. But he hadn't, so he didn't.

But what he had inadvertently done was open up the conversation to everyone else, who saw his comment as a kind of invitation to a forum of shit ideas.

'It could be for a locket!'

'Or a safety deposit thingy'

'Or a desk drawer'

'Or...'

'Or a post box'

'Or maybe some kind of wooden box!'

They all stopped. Nine eyes looked at the box.

Very slowly Franco moved his hand towards the centre of the table and Gaz slapped it down.

'It's not going to be a key to unlock the box that it's IN, is it Franco?'

'Oh. No. Ha. That would be silly'. Franco angled his head slightly anyway, just to see if the box had a lock.

'Franco!' Gaz snapped. Franco straightened his head up . 'It's not going to be a key to unlock the box that it's in, is it? Because...'

Franco thought for a bit.

'Come on, mate, you can do this.'

'Because... if the key locked the box, then how...'

'That's it, you're getting there'

'...how would you lock the key inside? And if it WAS locked inside...'

'Yes?'

'...how would you unlock it?'

'Well done!'

There was a general feeling of relief.

Dusty, who had never heard of a rhetorical question, let alone a paradox, said 'a crowbar!'

'What, Dusty?'

'Well if someone had used the key to lock the key in the box, you wouldn't be able to use the key to unlock it, would you? So you'd have to use a crowbar. Or a hammer, or maybe get some of those lock picking tools off the internet.'

'What if it's the key to someone's heart?'

There were murmurs of general agreement around the table, as if this was the kind of sensible suggestion that warranted murmurs of general agreement.

No, that's just a metaphor.' This was the first time Steven had spoken. Everyone listened when Steven spoke, because he used words like "metaphor" and didn't have a name that was a shortened version of another name. 'I don't think the keys to someone's heart are actual keys.'

'I'm sure I've heard of a person holding the key to someone's heart. Like, it was in a song or something.'

'Yes, and in another song, Elton John worked a plough on a farm. We can't go looking to songs for facts now, can we?' Steven winked playfully, although as far as everyone else was concerned he just made a weird expression with his mouth while some wrinkles formed behind the edges of his eye-patch. 'I expect there's something Mr Higgins isn't telling us.'

'Oh probably,' said Higgo. 'I haven't spoken to him for ages.'

'How IS your dad, Higgo?' Franco asked.

'Much better now, yeah. The gout in his foot was giving him all sorts of trouble, but he discovered that if he just sat watching telly all day it hardly hurt at all.'

Franco nodded thoughtfully. 'He's a clever man, your dad.'

'Sure is. Fixed his gout AND he's caught up on all the Father Brown mysteries.'

Steven cleared his throat. 'Why are we talking about your father?'

'I dunno, you mentioned him.'

'I most certainly did not.'

'Yeah,' said Dusty. 'You did. You said there was something Mr Higgins wasn't telling us.'

Steven opened his mouth as if to say something, but then decided against it. 'Quite right. So... Higgo, perhaps there is something else YOU are not telling us?'

'Well, I mean he also has irritable bowel, but I figured you didn't want to know that.'

'NOT ABOUT YOUR FATHER YOU INGNORAMUS!' Steven stopped. 'I apologise. This heat must be getting to me.'

Franco put up his hand. 'Perhaps we should sit down?'

'An excellent suggestion, Francis. Franco.'

They all sat down.

'So, Higgo. Tell us exactly what happened when you procured this key.'

Higgo started to look worried.

'Look, you're not in trouble. But understand, we sent you out on this errand in the hope that you would return with a solution, and you come back with... whatever this is.'

'It's a key.' Dusty was always one to stick with what he knew.

'With this key, yes. Now you say it's the key that will unlock... what was it?

'Un... unlock the answer to all of our problems. That's what the guy said, yeah.'

Gav piped in. 'What else did he say, Higgo? What else did the guy say?'

Steven put up his hand.

'Now now, Gav. How about we take it from the top, Higgo? Take us through the whole shebang.'

'OK. Okay, yeah. So it all went down like you said it would. I said I had come about the offer. They said "what offer?" just like they were supposed to, and I almost forgot what I had to say after that. But I thought about what Franco had said and that helped me remember. Cheers for that Franco.'

'You're welcome, son.'

'What did Franco say?'

'Never mind that, Gav. Keep going Higgo.'

'So they brought me inside, and I showed them the money. They went out the back, and then this guy came back. Dressed up real sharp. Like he was going to a funeral, or running a game show. And he's got this little box in his hand. He says "you're here about the offer?" and so I said "what offer?" cos I got a bit muddled, and thought we were doing that bit again but with the roles reversed. But he just laughed and laughed. Which is weird, cos I didn't even say the Franco thing.'

Franco laughed. 'Imagine if he was already thinking that?' Franco and Higgo laughed at the thought of this.

Gav was ramping up again. 'Thinking what? What did Franco say?'

Steven held up his hand again. 'It's really not important. Keep going. What happened next, Higgo?'

'After he stopped laughing he handed me the box. He said: "Don't open it until you get back to your compartments". I told him I lived in a house, and besides I was coming straight here.'

'Let me guess, that set him off laughing again, yes? I assume he actually said "compatriots", which means "people from your country, or your area". He meant us, you see? He knew that we were a group, and it's pretty obvious he's not from the same place as us, so that's what he meant.'

Higgo nodded. 'And what about the apartment?'

'Never mind that. What happened next, Higgo?' Gav asked.

'Well, I said "Is that it? Just this little box?" and he said - actually he sounded just like you Steven, he said "this little box is no ordinary little box. This little box will unlock the answer to all of your problems." Just like that. That's what he said. Then he gave me the receipt and I walked out.'

Gav's eyes opened wide. 'Wait, he gave you a receipt?'

'Well yeah, of course.' Higgo rolled his eyes. 'I bought this key off him. Of course he's going to give me a receipt. I mean, that's how buying stuff works, Gav.'

'What does it say?'

'I dunno. It's just a receipt. I mean, it's not like we can get a refund, so I didn't even look at it. I'm not even sure I kept it.'

'But you know it's a receipt.'

'What else would it be? I gave him money, he gave me the box, and a piece of paper. Of course it's a receipt.'

Gav was reaching his earlier peak. 'Give it. NOW.'

'Geesh, OK.' Higgo fished around in his pockets. From one pocket he pulled out a key ring, a crumpled-up paper bag from the local vegan donut shop and something that used to be sticky but was now furry. From his other pocket he pulled out a beer bottle cap, something that used to be furry but was now sticky, and a small folded piece of paper. He handed it to Gav, who had already started ranting while Higgo was on his fishing expedition.

'It's ONLY a receipt, he says. It's ONLY a normal piece of paper. Dammit Higgo, it could be a receipt, yes, or an instruction manual, even a little note! It could be literally anything, and you're just jamming it into your pocket like it's a piece of lettuce!'

At this, Dusty looked at Franco, and they silently and wisely decided to let that one slide.

After he snatched it from Higgo's hand, he unfolded it. 'Now. What do we have here? So it IS a receipt? The vendor at the top there. The customer, the Limbo group, that's us there. One item, "The key to heaven" and the amount we paid.' He turned the piece of paper over. 'That's it. That's all it says.'

'The key to what, Gav?'

'It says "the key to heaven". I don't get it.'

'I wonder,' said Dusty, 'if it's another one of them whats-it-fors?'

'A metaphor,' said Steven. 'Somehow I don't think it is.'

Steven looked around the room. The white, featureless, windowless, doorless, boundless room.

'I don't think it is.'

He stood up and reached over to pick up the key. As soon as he touched it, he disappeared.

Gav leant over, touched the key, and also disappeared.

Dusty looked at the receipt. 'How long have we been called the Limbo group? I thought we were called the Gavs.'

Franco and Higgo, simultaneously realising what was happening, also grabbed for the key and disappeared.

Dusty looked again at the receipt, and then around the now completely empty room. Finally he looked at the key. 'So it wasn't for a lock after all.'

Dusty grabbed the key and stepped into eternity.

ADULT EDUCATION, BY COLIN O'BRIAN
CHAPTER – THORNBURY, VIC

I don't know why Liam bothers with Father's Day gifts. Firstly, I'm 67 and he's 47. Secondly, I was a terrible father. I'm still a terrible father. Also, I hate gifts. But here I am standing behind some other decrepit old bastard who too would have been perfectly satisfied with a mug or pair of socks—hell, even a fucking card.

It's Wednesday night, a mist of rain falls gently, enough to wet the roads but not the hair. The other old bastard and I are in line at the Melbourne Centre for Adult Education waiting to be told where to go. I wish they'd tell me what I'm bloody doing here. It's an old building. Heavy rendering and even heavier layers of water-damaged ivory-coloured paint keep the weathered bricks from falling. The large and dimly lit walls provide the perfect canvas for someone called 'N8te-Dawg' to repeatedly write his name at different angles using paint from a can. Good one N8te-Dawg.

Liam thought it would be a good idea for me to learn how to use a computer and the internet. Happy Father's Day! He sold it to me with promises of convenient banking and news, along with a healthy dose of grandparent guilt - 'the kids can email you!' Little terrors can't even bloody read yet. Really, he just wants me to do something other than getting on the punt and enjoying a quiet drink with a select few. Liam was always a lot like his mother. According to Trav, a member of the select few, I can get on the punt using the internet, which sounds like a reasonable alternative for when the back, lungs or both can no longer get me to The Hawke.

The fella in front of me smells like firewood that's been soaked in Pine O Clean. He's wearing tan corduroy pants and a green and white polka-dotted shirt. He keeps adjusting his chequered flat cap and his glasses, alternating between the two like he can't find the right spot. I bet he doesn't own a TV. I feel like telling him that his clothes and glasses aren't hiding the gaping old-man-slouch of his back. Prick does look good, though. Smells like shit.

'Next please.'

The lady at reception lobs a smile at me that exceeds her hourly pay rate. Her name badge says Michelle. I tell Michelle I'm here for the course that teaches me how to punt on the internet. The smile doesn't budge a bloody millimetre.

'I'm afraid Mckay doesn't provide a course of that nature, sir. Do you have your booking reference number? It would have been emailed to your registered email address.'

Who the fuck is Mckay?

'Who is Mckay?' I say.

'The Melbourne Centre for Adult Education. It's just easier to say Mckay.'

That smile must be stitched permanently in place; I feel like I'm lined up at Luna bloody Park. It's a nice smile, though. It begins to sing to me like a siren. It says, 'yes the irony of an adult education centre using a half-assed and phonetically inaccurate acronym for its own name is not lost on me, but I've got HECS to pay, so I'll continue on smiling until that son of a bitch debt disappears'.

Her name badge is perfectly placed on her even more perfectly fitted polo shirt. Her ponytail is stretched back so tightly that each follicle is anchored nervously into her scalp. But her golden curls have escaped beyond the hair tie, free to roam. I wonder if Michelle and I could be lovers.

'It is easier to say,' I agree awkwardly.

'Yes. It is. Your booking reference number, sir?'

Bugger off Michelle, I'm trying to be personable. Liam says I need to work on my active listening skills and being more personable with people who aren't regulars at The Hawke. I suspect it's another reason he gave me this gift.

'I don't have an email address, that's what I'm here for. My son booked it for me,' I say.

'Your name, sir?'

I swear I saw the smile twitch as she said this. Her poker face breaking for a moment.

'As a gift,' I add for no reason. 'It's Glenn, double-n'.

'Surname?'

'Hemingway,' I reply, waiting for the response I usually receive.

'Ahh like the writer!' She says.

There it is. I hoped Michelle was better than this.

'Yeah, like the author, but one m,' I say, doing my best to be personable.

She tells me I'm in the Introduction to Personal Computers and the Internet course, which is in the Dewey Room, third door on the right down the passageway. It occurs to me that the room is probably named after the library system we used in school. Then it occurs to me that it never occurred to me that the system was named after someone. How hard was it to come up with 'how about whacking a few numbers on the spines of the books so people can find them?'

My nephew had a mate, I think his name was Paul, who placed a quaddie during his own wedding ceremony, hand in pocket flicking about on his mobile phone without taking his eyes off his bride. I think it was at the Valley, Cox Plate day. Bastard danced away with over 20 grand. Would have paid for the wedding, but he couldn't tell the wife. Apparently he still has the money, too scared to tell her how he got it. Forget the bloody Dewey system, try pulling off a Paul.

The carpet and fluorescent lights that lead to the Dewey Room are almost identical to the carpet and lights in the TAB at The Hawke. A mix of shades of green and navy blue, intertwining into royal-like crests framing red roses. Only difference is the time and care afforded to the cleanliness of the carpet and light in Mckay. It is easier to say 'Mckay'. Still, I begin to feel a little more comfortable in my current surroundings, a sense of familiarity alleviating the worries and general disdain of being here. I wonder who's at The Hawke tonight. It's Wednesday, pay-day for a few I'd say. Jim should be in fine form. He still owes me from last pay-day when he blew most of his hard earned on some long-shot multi. Jim's a great guy but a terrible punter. I've met his wife, so lending him a couple of hundred and saving his arse was the most charitable thing I've ever done. Tonight would have been a good night to recover that debt, especially after receiving a couple of strong tips from Gav on the second and fifth at the Bendigo trots. Lethal Leigh is paying 20s, and Gav says she can't lose. When Gav says something can't lose you'd miss your own kid's funeral to find the closest TAB.

The Dewey Room is brightly lit and smells like it is cleaned daily. An array of five rows of desks evenly spread, each containing five computers lay waiting. Whoever arranged room really wanted someone to notice their symmetrical work of art. Either that or they've missed a few OCD therapy sessions of late. A desk beside the entry is set up with name badges, also organised into a perfect array. Names are printed with a science-fiction themed font – someone has gone to a lot of trouble. There are ten left on the desk, including mine, and there are around 15 people already in the room, either sitting at a computer or milling around the tea and coffee station. Those already in the room chat politely, creating an even and consistent purr, not too dissimilar to happy hour in the front bar at The Hawke of a Friday afternoon.

I look for Pine O Clean man, but he isn't here. The smarmy bastard is probably signed up for a creative writing course or is learning a language - French or Spanish. I take my badge, place it in my pocket and make my way to the tea and coffee station to evaluate the biscuit selection. Monte Carlos, bloody beauty. I furtively glance either side of me before taking four and sitting down at a computer on the edge of the third row, which is closest to the exit. Others begin to do the same, minus the Monte Carlo stash, when a tall, slim man arrives at the front of the room. He's in his late thirties, has a messy curly mop of brown hair with greying sideburns. He wears a knitted vest over a blue shirt, sleeves rolled up to just below the elbows and tucked loosely into faded burgundy chinos. The colour of his eyebrows match his sideburns and bunch at the bridge of his nose, reaching for his forehead like a plant towards the sun. Without looking, he nonchalantly places some notes onto the table, opens a laptop and begins to plug in cords that extend from a hole in the table. He has a lapel microphone and his name badge says 'Malcolm'. Those still gathered chatting infer Malcolm's movements as a sign we're about to begin and take a seat at a computer. To my left sits a neatly-dressed woman in her fifties. She wears a yellow jumpsuit that flares at the legs. She wears it well. A large brown belt is wrapped around her waist like a newly crowned wrestling champion, and she stands tall in dark green thongs atop about 10 centimetres of platform. She smells of cigarette smoke and patchouli. I can only think of two reasons she would be here. The first that comes to mind is a meddling child who believes they know what's best for their mum. The second is she had to lay-off younger staff at her PR firm following the lock-downs and now realises she doesn't know shit about computers. She retrieves a notepad and pen from a designer handbag and it is at this point I notice that everyone in the room has various forms of notebooks, pens and pencils. I try to convince myself that stationery will not be necessary for the lesson, but I don't do a good enough job to do away with that unnerving feeling that comes with being the odd one out in a crowd.

Malcolm begins to speak. He introduces himself and his background working in computers, tells us where the emergency exits are located, when there will be breaks and something about an issue with the toilet, but I hardly register anything he says. Shit, Liam you shit, you didn't say anything about bloody notepads! I control my thoughts and remind myself that I don't want to be here and I don't care about computers nor the internet. A chuckle escapes from me. Yellow jumpsuit lady hastily turns her head to me, revealing almond-shaped grey eyes, then just as quickly adjusts her face to a polite smile of acknowledgement. My eyes, ears and mind return to Malcolm.

'Many thanks to everyone for completing the pre-course material,' Malcolm says. 'Turning on a computer may seem simple; however, it can stump people, but I prefer to get these things out of the way before our first session so we can launch straight into the nitty-gritty.'

Shit, Liam, you shit.

'Looking around the room, I can see that many of you, if not all of you have brought your login details for the course,' Malcolm continues, tapping the knife a little further in. 'If you don't have this with you, it was emailed with the pre-course material, but Michelle can provide you with a copy at the front desk.'

The knife lodges a little further in. The same knife I'm going to use to fucking murder fucking Liam.

'Can everyone please turn their computer on and login using these details,' Malcolm continues to say. It's a bit bloody stupid emailing so much information to a group of people learning how to use a computer. What email did Liam even use for my registration?

I inspect the Dewey Room for another poor lost soul, an ally in unpreparedness, naivety or ignorance; I'll take anything. From my vantage point I see no such comrade. Bugger this. Time to swallow the pride and get the details from Michelle. Firstly, let's turn this computer on. How do I do that? There isn't a blasted on button anywhere I can see, and it's too late to watch someone else do it - everyone in the room has already turned their damn thing on. I can't ask Malcolm; he'll know I didn't do the pre-course reading. Change of plan. Michelle first then find the on button. I rise from my chair without thinking, creating what seems like a cacophony of chairs and desks being dragged along a recently polished floor. Heads turn to me like I bloody-well farted.

'Everything okay...' Malcolm strains his eyes to read my name badge. 'Sir?' he settles with, giving up on his needless attempts to see my badge which isn't there.

'Glenn,' I reply.

'Sorry Glenn, couldn't see your badge from here. Can I help you with something?'

Yes Malcolm, you could start with telling me how the fuck I turn this computer on, then you can give me the login details, and while you're at it, kill my son and give me the winners for Rosehill this weekend, you prick.

'All good, just need the loo,' I lie.

'Michelle will give you the key and directions,' he says.

'The what?'

'As I said at the beginning, the internal toilets are out of order, but we have access to one outside, just needs a key, which Michelle has,' Malcolm says with an undertone of annoyance.

'Yes, of course, thank you, be right back,' I say apologetically without actually feeling or being sorry.

I can't get out of this room fast enough. My decision to sit next to the exit turns out to be a masterful act of foreshadowing.

I retrace my steps back to Michelle's desk and ask for the keys to the toilet. Michelle hands me a single key attached to a hunk of plastic that could be used to a play a decent game of totem tennis. Her directions to the toilet are convoluted and seem unnecessary. I listen but don't pay attention.

'I can show you the way if you like?' Michelle offers. Her ponytail hasn't budged, nor has her smile.

'I'm sure I'll be right,' I say.

Despite not needing the loo, I figure I may as well go, anything to keep up the charade. I walk out of Mckay and turn left past N8te-Dawg and turn left again down a narrow alleyway. It's as dark as you would expect an alleyway to be, but darker than a public toilet should be. Michelle mentioned re-entering the building and some right turns; I can't recall the order of the turns. An architect would lose consciousness or the will to live if they saw the absurd labyrinth of doors scattered along the side of this building. I decide to try the only door with any semblance of light sneaking through the gaps. It's a storeroom, and I don't dare check what's on the other side of its internal door. I then decide to try every door. None are toilets. What am I doing? I don't even need the toilet and enough time has passed since I left the Dewey Room for it to be an uncomfortable return, that's if I can even find my way back.

Fuck it. I'm leaving.

As I retrace my steps back through the toilet-less maze, I rehearse some lies to feed Liam as to why I didn't attend – something COVID-based the short-priced favourite. I am comforted by the sight of N8te-Dawg's wall and toss the keys to the mystery loo into a neglected garden running lengthways along the wall.

It's 8pm. The Hawke is a 20-minute taxi ride away. Lethal Leigh runs at 8:40pm.

I open my wallet and check there's enough for the taxi with a little extra for the punt. I calculate that if I get the driver to drop me off a little earlier, about a ten minute walk away, I'll have enough time to lay the bet and have about an extra tenner to place for the win. Jim should still be there. It's a good chance to get that money back. He should be in fine form by now.

POWERBALL, BY HOWARD RALLEY
CHAPTER – YARRAVILLE, VIC

The TV presenter had a million-dollar smile in a one-dollar job. Presenting the weekly Powerball result wasn't exactly the career choice she had in mind when she was back studying journalism. But screw it, she thought to herself. 'A gig's a gig,' as her Dad used to say.

Facing the camera, ridiculously overdressed, and looking like a surprise guest at a wedding, she stood in the middle of two oversized fish-bowls and made her eyes sparkle as she read through the brief script.

'Good evening and welcome to this evening's Powerball draw number 1377.' She glanced down as the first fish-bowl fired up and started the little blue balls dancing.

Eyes back to the camera. 'And if you win tonight's Division One Powerball this could be the start of a whole new life.'

A flash of that smile, a flare of the eyebrows, a left shoulder slightly forward, a suggestion we were best pals. Maybe we could work together here?

'The total tonight for one lucky winner is a whopping $61 million,' and she bit her bottom lip in excitement. 'And the first number tonight is—'

The camera pans to the little light-filled piston that raises one ball from out of the dance. The ball is raised to the top of the dome, like a priest holding up the blood of Christ. The ball is tipped into a little funnel and as it rolls, the number is tantalizingly unreadable, until at last, it bumps to rest and sits on display.

'—Number 28,' she calls out. 'Is that one of your life-changing numbers?'

***

William leaned back in his bath feeling proud of himself. At 2.30 in the afternoon on a Tuesday, his hobby of decadent bath times was going well. Surely, he smiled to himself, no one else in this shitty High-Rise was having a bath right now? He friggin owned this.

He slipped further down into the bath and was rewarded by a little wave of warm water. For a moment, the two bobbing little yellow rubber ducks were in perfect balance. A universe in sync. Like when you're at the traffic lights and your car indicators match the guys in front. But timing is everything, William thought to himself, and these moments rarely last long. The water soon settled, and the ducks broke their alliance, turning in separate directions.

An urgent rap at the bathroom door broke his thoughts.

It was his girlfriend, Jay.

'Holy fuck Will,' she called out. 'My waters just, like, broke. No shit. For real. So, yeah, it's game on.' There was a sense of rising panic from behind the door.

William stared at the rubber ducks. They stared back. He couldn't think of what to say. He opted for facts.

'I'm in the bath,' he said, feeling stupid.

'No shit Sherlock. Who takes a fucking bath on a Tuesday afternoon? Unless you think we have a shit ton of towels, you better grab the car keys. This baby is coming.'

William's brain at last kicked in. He sat bolt up in the bath sending the ducks on a roller coaster. OK, OK, get Jay to the hospital, we can do this, he told himself. Timing was everything.

'And don't forget my lucky house key,' she called out.

***

'And tonight's second and third number is...42 and 17', her voice as warm as Christmas Eve. 'So far we have 28, 42 and 17. And,' her eyes widened, 'we're not far away from tonight's all-important Powerball number...'

***

Jay tried to remember her breathing exercises as the car pushed through the mid-day traffic. William was hunched over the wheel in furious concentration. She rolled her eyes. For the next year, he'll be banging on about how great a job he did getting to the hospital.

The wipers didn't work, and spots of rain were appearing on the windscreen, each drop first wobbling and then stretching out and streaking with each acceleration. She felt the same, wrung out and stretched out of shape.

She cursed herself. How many times had she nagged him about the wipers? 'We'll be right,' he'd said two months ago when they got the $360 quote to fix it. No way could they pay for it. 'We'll just drive in the summertime!' he laughed.

The contractions were getting stronger. The dull ache in the lower back growing sharper. She felt it through her legs. For some reason, her mind thought of Sauron's Tower in Mordor, flashes of lightning and flaming vaginas. Of dark days to come. She caught herself about to gasp from the pain. She managed to turn it into a kind of loud sigh. Where did that come from? This breathing exercise stuff was bullshit.

'Drugs,' she said out loud to the windscreen. 'Lots of drugs.'

Her Mum had said once that things get honest when the pain kicks in. It was about the only semi-wise thing she remembers her saying. Wise words from a hospital bed after another failed attempt to get off the booze. 'Gin-clear clarity' she called it...

Jay flipped down the sun visor and examined her puffy eyes. She was going to be better Mum, she'd told herself. She may not have wanted this baby, but by God, she was going to work hard at being the best goddamn Mum on the planet. Just need some money. Always the money.

Another contraction. The pain ripped through her. She gripped her lucky house key tighter. She tried to recall their little caravan just off the Ring Road. It was the first place they ever had. A dump, but it was theirs. You could walk its entire length in 4 strides. After shots, they'd play "The floor is lava" and end up in a heap laughing. They were only there for five months before their big move to the Flats. But they were happier back then. Should have stayed, she thought to herself.

As the wave of another cramp began to rise and dark clouds gathered over Mordor, she gripped the edge of the car seat and started once again with the 4-7-8 breathing technique.

***

It better not rain. It better not rain. It better not rain. William drove in silence and prayed and prayed to beat the rain clouds. You couldn't say they were just rain spots on the windscreen now. I mean, it wasn't raining. More of a drizzle. A light shower? Fuck.

He could almost reach out and touch the waves of judgement coming from Jay. She made a loud sigh. Yep, right there. Judgy. Christ, it better not rain. One job. Get to the hospital. He'll never live it down if they had to get an uber or something.

Still, he'd made some great driving decisions so far. That Coles truck was way behind him now, almost out of sight. He sucked at pretty much most things, but give him a gap in the traffic and he was your man. It was about being decisive, see. Like when he took control and they moved to the Flats.

A new thought occurred to him. He'll teach his kid how to drive, sure he will. Handing down skills, father to son and all that. How good would that be, he smiled. And he wouldn't be one of those helicopter parents who jumped out of their skin at every mistake. No, he'd be like, chill, don't worry, screwing up is how you learn. And then they would both break out into The Beatles and start singing together "With every mistake we must surely be learning". He'd take the kid over to a Bunnings carpark early Sunday morning and they could have the run of the place. They would laugh at the dents in the car.

A question occurred to him. He looked over at Jay. 'Hey, reckon the Bunnings carpark at Altona is bigger than the one at HighPoint?' he asked.

She didn't answer. He chuckled at himself. The kid isn't even born yet and I'm planning driving lessons.

Boy or girl, didn't matter to him. They had agreed not to ask the obstetrician. He'd said to Jay at the time, let's keep the surprise huh? He almost fell off his chair when she agreed. She normally wants to know everything.

Still, it kinda made painting the nursery hard. He went for yellow. He had read somewhere that people are more likely to wake up in good moods in a yellow bedroom. His mates gave him shit for that one.

The Dulux card said it was called 'bumblebee'. He got the non-branded paint, saved some cash, but it came out a bit mustard. Jay said he should have painted a sample first. But he wanted it done and was excited about the whole big reveal.

He'd put his hands over Jay's eyes and frog-marched her to the doorway of the nursery. You couldn't have done that in a caravan. She cried when she saw it. They hugged and then held hands looking at the Ikea cot all ready and waiting. He remembered they stood in happy silence, each lost in their thoughts.

***

The presenter's smile was fixed as she kept the commentary steady. 'And tonight, you'll need the numbers 6 and 15 to go with the first three numbers'. Her voice lowered as if she was sharing a secret, 'and remember if there is no winner tonight the jackpot will rise to $80 million in next week's draw. So, make sure you grab your Powerball ticket each week.'

***

The contractions were next level. Jay struggled to sit still. She couldn't breathe. She needed to move. She squirmed in the car seat, the seat belt brutal against her body. Literally, where were the lungs supposed to go, she complained to herself. She felt the baby kick. She kept squeezing the house key, its metallic edge digging into her palm. The hospital wasn't far now, a few more blocks. Each red light was keeping her from drugs. Could Will drive any slower, she cursed. He was driving like the Queen's undertaker. Precious cargo on board. For fucks sake just floor it, she thought.

He looked over at her and asked her something about a Bunnings carpark. Seriously? For a moment she just looked at his face, all eager for an answer, before turning away speechless. Incredulous, that was the word. Fucking incredulous. Maybe he was on the drugs?

'Are you singing The Beatles?' she asked.

'Just, y'know, it came to mind.' He made a stupid grin.

'Can you not?'

She was being mean, she knew it. He was a good guy. He was getting her to the hospital, right? He wasn't trophy boyfriend material, but he was kind. Hell, she wasn't exactly a trophy girlfriend herself. He meant well. He wasn't that handy around the place, and he was on minimum wage, but he didn't get angry, he didn't give her a hard time, and he loved her, that much she knew.

She wouldn't mind their boy having some of that kindness. She had called back the obstetrician and asked for the gender. No way was she going to be in the dark for seven months. She felt bad not telling Will. But it had helped Jay to come to terms with this stranger growing inside her.

When she told Will she was pregnant he was shocked but then picked her up and spun her around. He rushed out and got some Prosecco in to celebrate. Then told her not to drink any while he got happily drunk. He apologised the next morning. He was good at that, accepting when he was in the wrong, quick to give her space.

But then again, the kid might not inherit any of that. After all, Will wasn't the father. It didn't matter, she told herself, staring at the next set of traffic lights as the rain picked up, and feeling like she was going to cry.

She made herself shift her thoughts to the pragmatic. He can repaint the nursery when they get home. Bless him. Only Will could paint something vomit-coloured and think it was OK. In her way, she did love him. She knew it. Loved him enough anyways.

Another contraction crashed over her. She screwed up her eyes and blew air through pursed lips. A silent tune William could never hear.

***

William swung the car into the hospital carpark and found a parking spot on Level 1.

'Bingo!' he said with a whoop. He jogged round to the passenger side and helped Jay out.

They fumbled their way out of the car, over to the lift, waited for an eternity, and got to the labour ward as another contraction hit.

William admired how the nurses asked short sharp questions to Jay. No nonsense, no wasted words. Jay answered equally matter of fact. Don't come to this Ward for small talk, he thought to himself.

Things moved fast and William found himself on the periphery of things. He asked a couple of questions to look keen, but no one heard. At one of those pre-natal classes a few months back they had shared a joke about playing whale music.

'But whale music would freak me out,' she'd laughed.

'How about otters?' he said randomly, and it had become a thing ever since. William thought he might try his luck.

'Hey, is it time for the otter music?' he half laughed in Jay's direction. She didn't seem to have heard. Fair enough, he thought to himself, rinsing his hands.

A midwife turned to him, a warm Dublin accent. 'A good cup of tea would be the thing,' she said, 'not too hot mind.' And he left the room.

In the waiting room, William found a kettle and some teabags. There was a little white bowl with a sign saying 'for utensils', but someone had put a used T-bag in it. Probably had bigger things on their mind.

The room smelt of too-strong cleaning products. You don't need disinfectant for a coffee table, he thought.

He looked around. Three other guys sat in the room, all on their phones. No one looked up.

A sudden thought. He reached for his phone and texted his Dad: 'GAME ON. AT HOSPITAL' and then, 'ALL OK'.

Time dragged. There wasn't much to look at. In the top left-hand corner by the corridor, a TV was fixed to the wall. One of those cheap flat-screen TV's that you struggled to see at an angle. It was some crap channel, showing the Powerball draw. An overdressed presenter was smiling at the camera and reading the video prompt about the next number being a lucky number.

Despite himself, he watched the little blue ball roll down the hamster chute, and bounce to a stop next to the others. Number 4. Hey, that was their caravan number, he'd have put that one down.

He had finished his tea, then made a fresh one for Jay and headed back to her room. Cries were coming from inside. William hoped the tea wasn't too hot.

***

The cheap graphics and row of numbers had almost filled the screen and the presenter was nearing the end of the show.

'And so, let's have a recap on tonight's winning numbers. We have 28, 42, 17, 6, 15, the number 4 and now,' a pause, 'and now, the last of the regular numbers, lucky number 30.'

***

William felt that something was wrong as soon as he walked into the room. The obstetrician was on his way apparently, coming straight in. There were too many people around. Five of them. Who were all these people? Jay was like a cornered animal scrunched up hard against the head of the bed. She was covered in sweat, wild-eyed, and screaming for drugs. The midwives were calling for her to push, to bear down, asked if she would put her legs in stirrups. Jay made it clear that wasn't going to happen.

William discarded the stupid tea to one side and rushed to Jay. She grabbed his arm and pulled him close.

'What's happening?' she whispered, looking into his eyes. She held his stare. He fell inside it, pulled in by an undiluted fear.

'I'm here,' he whispered back, 'I'm here. You're amazing. It's OK. It's all going OK.'

He tried to make a small joke. What an adventure huh? The laugh rattled around his body like a fly trying to escape an upturned glass. The joke soon ran out of air.

She grimaced in pain.

'I'll do you a deal" he whispered again, 'we'll swap places, yeah?' He smiled.

For a moment her eyes smiled back. 'OK,' she said softly, 'Yes, I'd like that.' Then she vanished again under another wave.

William looked over and could see a tiny trickle of blood from her right that clenched the key, still in her hand.

***

A nurse, the Irish one, called out to the others.

'I don't know but? It's not crowning see?'

And then to Jay, 'But come on now Jay, we need you. Come on now, push for me, Jay--'

William heard how he was using her name a lot. Joined in. 'You're doing great babe, brilliant Jay.'

And then a flurry of activity. Alarm bells on machines that looked designed from the 1980s.

Everyone in the room had a job to do. Not William. He stayed with Jay. He cradled her burning cheek with his left hand as his right was held in a vice-like grip by Jay. He stayed with her eyes as the nurse's commentary came in fits and starts.

'OK now. That's it.'

I don't know what, well, I don't think...'

'Keep pushing Jay. You're doing great Jay...'

And then a stop. Everything stopped. The room fell silent. Just the blinking of a monitor.

As if rehearsed, all five nurses took a single step back. A nurse put her gloved hands to her mouth. One of them reminded William of that kid in Home Alone. They stared down.

One stepped forward.

'It's...it's a slip of, of, it's a slip of paper?'

The Irish nurse joined her. 'Would you look at that now?' her voice high.

Jay made a last cry and fell back in exhaustion onto the bed, still holding her lucky key.

One of the nurses reacted first, grabbed a towel, and reached down to make the final pull, gently tugging at the paper. She held it close and used the towel to wipe a bit of blood from the left corner.

'It's a bloody lottery ticket, is what it is,' the nurse said.

The room was silent.

Jay, in a small voice, 'Can I hold it?'

The nurse wrapped the towel tighter and handed it up. Jay tucked it up close into the nook of her elbow and held it up close to her tear-stained cheek.

Another nurse, leaning half in the room and half out into the corridor was squinting over to the little TV in the waiting room. 'I can't see at this angle, hang on' and she disappeared.

She was back in a flash. '28, 42, 17, 6, 15, err, 4 and 30.'

William looked down at Jay and then at the little ticket. 'Holy fuck.'

Jay broke her eye contact with the ticket and looked up. 'What about the Powerball?'

The nurse at the door disappeared again and quickly returned. 'Number 11?'

Jay smiled. 'Course it is,' and tilted her arm upwards so that everyone in the room could see the ticket more clearly, half buried in the towel. 'Isn't it beautiful?' she asked to a stunned room.

***

Four hours later Jay was laying still and on her back. She opened her eyes slowly. The room took a moment to come into focus. She turned her head to the left. There was her Will holding a tiny baby bundled in a blue towel. William was gently shifting his weight, rocking sideways like it was the most natural motion in the world. She could see that he was holding the smallest hand she had ever seen.

William looked up. 'Hey there,' he says, voice all choked, 'isn't she beautiful?'

Jay turned her head away to hide her face. Tears started to fall. She noticed she still somehow held her lucky key and, relaxing her hand, she let it drop to the floor.

William noticed and stood puzzled. He stopped rocking. He doesn't know why but he suddenly recalled the little rubber ducks in his bath earlier. How they bobbed together briefly before turning in separate directions.

HIGHLY COMMENDED

THE DRAWER, BY ADRIEN BONNETTO
CHAPTER — CAULFIELD, VIC

Chapter 1

Kate walked back and forth on the footpath. She stared across the street at the house and checked her phone for the tenth time. Finally, the text she had been eagerly awaiting arrived. It was her brother Jack.

"So sorry sis, I'll be 45min late."

She clenched her teeth lightly as a puff of warm air escaped her mouth. She found it hard to contain her exasperation and hit the redial button on her phone instantly.

"Seriously? You know I can't do it by myself Jack! You promised!" Kate said.

"Sorry sis. There's an emergency at work. I'm doing my best believe me".

"But I'm already here." Kate said. "Richard will be back from work in 2 hours. What if he comes back when we are inside?"

Kate frowned struggling to keep her frustration in check. She wanted to do it today, but not alone.

"Technically, it's still your house, you have the keys. All you need is 30 mins to get your stuff. You'll be gone before he returns." Jack said.

"I don't know. It's too risky and I have a bad feeling." Kate said. She looked at the house again. It was still the same suburban house she had lived in for the last 4 years. "Maybe I'll leave it for today".

"What are you talking about?" said Jack. "You still have your valuables in there, our family photos and Mum's jewellery. These are the only things left of her."

"I know" Kate sighed. "Maybe I could just talk to him. He sent a message yesterday and apologised again. I'm not defending him, but he was really stressed and—"

Jack interrupted her. He closed his eyes trying to bring all his energy to find the right words, the right tone. He believed today would be different, but he realised history was going to repeat itself.

"You stop right there! Richard beat you and it was not the first time. Sorry to be blunt sis but you deserve better and you need to move on. You said it yourself this morning."

Jack continued: "It's okay, you don't need to take everything. You just want the valuable items. Then you get out. Easy"

Kate paused. The certainty of this morning was fading away.

"I can't do it for you Kate." Jack said. She could count on one hand the number of times he called her Kate. It was always sis. 'Kate' had always a serious tone attached to it.

"Okay, okay, I'll go" she finally said.

"I'll keep my phone on speaker next to me just in case you need my help. When it's over I'll arrange a nice day trip to the Mornington Peninsula Hotsprings. What do you say?"

She pondered for a while.

"Fine, I'll take you up on that offer. You'd better add a full-body massage!"

"Deal! I'm right here". Jack positioned the phone next to his desktop as Kate crossed the street.

Chapter 2

She opened the front door and entered. She could picture herself leaving in tears only ten days ago. She passed the living room where she had chosen the blue cushions that elevated the grey of the sofa. She had found vintage frames and created a mosaic of photos in the hallway. And yet she couldn't shake the feeling she was entering someone else's place. She had moved in with Richard, with love and dreams, and had left with nothing but a black eye and a broken heart. She walked directly upstairs to the bedroom, checked her drawers, opened the wardrobe, and looked at the bedside table. Everything was there, waiting for her.

In the bathroom, was her toothbrush, her organic creams and a bottle of her favourite shampoo and conditioner. The reflection in the mirror was looking back at her. There was judgement and a faint black eye. "It's still your home", she thought.

"Stop!" she said with her hand heavily anchored on the sink and her saddened face close to the mirror.

She wanted to give herself a pep talk but her words felt fake, like in a bad soap opera.

She looked at the bathroom for a few seconds. She hated when she couldn't decide what to do. Slowly she returned to the bedroom, opened the bag she had brought and started packing her shoes, some of her favourite clothes, expensive bags and belts, photos and notes.

She did not want to pack her life in a small bag. Her eyes welled up and she felt so miserable in that moment.

The harsh buzz of the doorbell startled her and brought her back to reality. She felt an electric current pass through her body from head to toe. The next instant, the door creaked as it opened, and a soft voice called: "May I come in?".

Chapter 3

Anna was the type of woman who made heads turn. She always made sure of that. Her skin was flawless, and her deep blue eyes were accentuated by her fake eyelashes. She always wore bright red lipstick. She was captivating.

She took her phone from her Chanel handbag and called as she approached the house.

"Hello handsome," she said.

"Hello beautiful. I'm so happy to hear from you again," said Richard already aroused by the impromptu call.

"It seems someone had a good time." She said while biting her lower lip.

"Well, it's been a while since I had such an ... interesting evening. You're quite an amazing woman."

He adjusted his headphones while enjoying the sensual act that had started.

"This is a delicate situation as I am not wearing much and it's a little crisp outside" whispered Anna as she pressed the doorbell.

"You would not leave a damsel in distress outside? Your door is already open. May I come in?"

"Sorry Anna," Richard was frowning. "Where are you? Are you at my place?"

" Yes, I am, but I get from your tone that you're not. So, my surprise has failed. Will you come back soon for another interesting evening?" Anna asked provocatively.

"Ooh, I wish I was there, believe me. I get home late on Thursdays." Richard confessed.

"Sorry but, did you say the door was open?" asked an anxious Richard as he realised what she had just said.

"Yes," said Anna. "But if you're not coming back soon, I'll just leave. "

"Wait, wait!" He took care choosing his words. "Could you do me a favour and go upstairs to check a drawer in my study?" There was a palpable sense of panic in his voice.

"Why? Should I be worried the door was open?" Anna was already walking away from the house into the front yard.

"No, no please, I probably forgot to lock the door this morning, but could you do me a favour and check the drawer."

"Geez, why are you stressed? I'm not going inside if you think the house has been broken into Richard," said Anna.

"Please, if you do that for me, I'll take you out shopping on Collins Street. What do you say?"

"You think you can bribe me?"

"Shall we say, this Saturday at 2 pm?" asked Richard, trying to maintain his composure.

Richard waited for an answer. If needed, he was ready to leave work immediately.

He continued, "I'm not asking you to check the whole house, just one drawer, upstairs. For my piece of mind. Please?"

"Alright I'm making my way upstairs, but Saturday better be good," she said.

They had just met a few weeks ago and had bonded instantly. She knew he had a partner, but she didn't seem to care. After all, she did not commit to anything and if he was keen to see someone else, it was not a problem for her.

"I promise. You're the best," said Richard.

"So, what do you want me to check? Asked Anna.

"The bottom drawer of my desk"

Anna teased him. "Someone has dark secrets it seems. What will I find in there, drugs, dirty money, what's your crime, Richard?"

"No nothing like that, it's just personal stuff, important memories, but better be safe than sorry". This was not his best performance.

"Yes, your drawer is fine. It's locked.

"Thanks a lot."

"Do you want me to do anything else while I'm here? I could just remove what I have on and keep chatting with you," said Anna.

"That sounds very - "

He did not finish his sentence. A text message had just appeared on his phone. He had been expecting it since the morning, and yet the reaction was immediate. Pearls of cold sweat formed on his forehead and the words became dry in his throat.

"I'm sorry Anna. I must go; I've got a meeting. I'll be in touch later and will see you on Saturday, promise."

[Tonight, 8pm at East Richmond station. 30k cash as agreed]

He took a deep breath and turned to a colleague.

"I have to leave, I'm not feeling well", he said.

"Yes sure, no worries," the other replied while staring at his screen.

Richard wanted the nightmare to stop. Soon he would be back home, he would pay back what he owed to the loan shark and his problems would be over. This weekend, he would spend a nice afternoon with

Anna and a pleasurable evening too. If possible, he would also get Kate to listen to him and she would come back. Perfect.

Chapter 4

Kate's heart was pounding out of her chest. Her flight or fight response overrode her body, and she froze. The sound of her breath was raspy and uneven. The doorbell had resonated into the house like never before and a woman was now downstairs, flirting on the phone with Richard.

Kate did not move. Her brain rebooted.

"You've been cheated on, don't you be so stupid!" she thought. This was classic Kate, soft with others and a bully towards herself. She was sobbing quietly in her bedroom.

The woman downstairs was apparently leaving. As Kate regained her senses, she went to the bedroom window to glimpse at a tall bimbo, in a trench coat and high heels leaving the house and stopping at the front gate.

She dried her tears and remembered Jack was still on the phone.

"Jack, someone just came into the house!"

"What? Is it Richard?"

"No, it's a woman, Richard is". She paused as the words formed in her throat "I think he's cheating on me." said Kate in a quavering voice.

"Shit, Jack, she's back, what do I do, what do I do?"

"Hide, hide somewhere in the wardrobe or under the bed".

Kate took the bag, threw it under the bed and crawled next to it.

"What's happening?" asked Jack.

"Shh" whispered a terrified Kate.

'You always make bad decisions. You should have never come back", she thought to herself.

In no time, two long and beautifully curved legs appeared in the corridor and entered the study.

Kate listened to the conversation. The dusty carpet was tickling her nose and its roughness was irritating her cheek. The sexual banter between the two removed the slightest doubt she might have had that Richard had cheated on her. She felt sick as she discovered the truth about his affair while hiding under her own bed. The humiliation hit her like a slap in the face. She had given everything to Richard, she had put her heart and soul into their relationship.

Why was that woman checking a drawer? It didn't make any sense. She remembered that Richard never liked it when she was in his study. Whatever was in that drawer was important. She made up her mind.

Chapter 5

"Sis are you there?" Jack said. It had been a few minutes since the woman had left the house. Jack's voice resonated far away in her head while she extracted herself from under the bed and sat on the floor. She removed the dust from her pants with shaking hands. She explained everything to Jack.

"I need to open that drawer."

"Sis, I get it's painful and you're probably in shock but don't do it. He'll know it was you. It will cause more trouble. Just leave".

"Easy for you to say". She was screaming at the phone. Her anger erupted like steam out of a boiling kettle.

"I know that nothing good will come out of you staying and seeking revenge now. It's not you".

"I don't want to be me." She paused for a few seconds. "I'll call you back later" and she hung up.

Jack tried to call back, but she had left her phone on the bed. She walked into the study, she shook the drawer and tried to force it open. She kicked it and swore at it. She searched for the key in every place she could think of. She opened the other drawers, lifted the various papers spread on the desk. She searched under the paper holder and even checked the silver tiger statue that was proudly roaring in the middle. She always had an immense dislike for that statue. Its purchase had led to their first fight.

She searched everywhere and still no key. She looked at her watch, 15 minutes had already passed. The tips of her ears were burning, and her head was throbbing. She paused and tried to think of other possibilities. She went back into the bedroom and opened his bedside table. The books she found there said a lot about Richard. They reminded her of his gambling issues. She almost missed the puzzle box that was hiding at the very back of the drawer. She shook it and there was something inside. She tried to recall the many times she saw Richard fiddle with it. She dug deep in her memories and finally after several tries, she twisted a corner and pushed on one side and the box gave in.

Inside was a small key. She rushed back to the study, inserted it into the drawer and it turned with a click. The drawer opened.

Chapter 6

Kate returned to the bedroom, picked up the phone and rang Jack.

"What the hell? What are you doing? Are you still there?"

"I opened the drawer" replied Kate.

"You're still there?"

"There is 30,000 dollars in cash!" she said.

"30 grand! No one has that amount of cash anymore! This stinks."

"I could really use it," said Kate. I deserve it!", she shouted.

"No, please, this is a bad idea. He will know it was you, and it will not end well. Just leave," pleaded Jack.

"This is my chance for revenge"

"This is a very bad decision, Kate."

This is a bad decision. The words resonated in her head.

"Isn't that what you make all the time? Bad decisions?" she thought. But this was too great an opportunity.

And in all this chaos, she remembered something. Richard was a gambler and very often lost it all. He asked his friends and when that was no longer enough, he got loans but not from the bank.

"Promise me you'll leave the money," said Jack.

"Okay I won't take the money, but I have an idea," said Kate.

"But first I need to leave everything I packed. Richard can't ever know I was here."

Chapter 7

Richard had packed and left work in a hurry. It had been bumper to bumper on the freeway as usual and he was now turning into his street. He parked the car in the garage and went directly to the front door. He was sure he had locked it this morning. He was still unsettled and decided to check upstairs for himself. Everything seemed fine. He picked up the key from his puzzle box and opened the drawer. The envelope was still here with the cash he owed. He felt an immense sense of relief but at the same time he couldn't shake the feeling that something was not quite right.

Had Kate come back to the house today? She had mentioned she wanted to pick up her things. He tried to call her, but it went straight to voice-mail. He went through her stuff and nothing seemed to have moved.

"I probably forgot to lock the door after all", he thought.

He glanced at his watch, it was the time for him to head to East Richmond station. He took the envelope and made his way to his car. It would all be over soon.

Chapter 8

Kate had emptied the bag and had placed everything back. She only took her mum's jewellery, and she knew that would go unnoticed by Richard.

She was staring at the cash, spread out on the desk. She remembered a few years ago, Richard coming back home with blood on his collar, puffed-up lips and an eye half closed. He had asked her for some cash explaining he owed money but that the bank had made a mistake and he was short. Each time she had tried to discuss this with him, it ended in a fight.

She carefully placed the money back into the drawer and locked it. She contemplated the desk and smiled at what she had done.

She would never have been able to pull such a big trick. It was not much but it was enough for her. She left the room feeling a little less bitter.

She took her bag and went downstairs, pausing to look at the house for the last time.

A loud noise suddenly resonated in the house. The garage door was opening giving off its very loud metallic sound. Richard was back. It was way too soon.

She rushed to the front window to see Richard turning into the driveway. She heard the engine turn off. She was shaking like a leaf but now was not the time to be paralysed by fear. The garage door hitting the ground was her cue to dash to the front door and hide behind the bins in the front yard. Her breath was out of control and her heart close to bursting out of her chest. The front door opened, and Richard went outside and gazed at the street. She held her breath until he went back inside.

Those 10 minutes she hid felt like hours. "Move, please move, please", she was screaming inside her head. She was cursing Jack for not being there with her like he promised. Gathering her last bit of strength, she stood up, dashed into the street and ran. As she reached the end of the street she turned and collapsed against a fence. She looked back desperately trying to see if she had been followed.

Her phone vibrated; Richard was calling.

"Shit, Shit, Shit!" She thought she was in the clear but the possibility that he knew felt like his hand around her throat. "He knows, I'm as good as dead". There was no way she was going to take that call.

She called Jack as soon as she reached the station, and recounted what just happened.

"Wow wait, calm down, take a deep breath. Are you safe? Tell me you are out of there", Jack asked.

"Yes. I'm at the train station."

"Okay, so Richard returned, did he see you?"

"No, I don't think so, I'm not sure."

"Did you take the money?"

"No, I didn't! It's still there."

"Good I am glad you didn't touch it."

"Well...", she hesitated.

"What have you done?" said Jack.

Chapter 9

On the way home, Richard was smiling and humming the tune that was playing on the radio. Everything went smoothly. After meeting them, he gave them the bag, and they left immediately. He was glad the exchange happened at the train station and not in some obscure back alley.

He came back home and poured a glass of red wine feeling relieved it was finally over. He was determined to turn his life around this time. He ordered his dinner from UberEats. He had time to squeeze in a relaxing shower before the order arrived. His bad luck was over, and he needed to celebrate.

His phone vibrated in his pocket.

[2k missing. You thought we wouldn't check? We will need 5k now for the trouble]

He froze, he understood the message, but it did not make any sense. He gave them the full amount.

The phone rang, same number. He answered and stuttered

" I gave you $30k. I swear. I have the receipts from the ATM. I did it over several days just as you asked."

"You think we don't know how to count? If we are telling you 2k is missing, then it is missing. You owe 5K now. Do you understand?"

His legs failed him, and he started to feel nauseous. It was a nightmare.

"I swear guys, I gave you the full amount. Maybe the bank made a mistake?"

"Well too bad, we will need to see the money"

"But I don't have it, I don't!" he said.

"It is fine, we understand - "and the line was cut.

"Hello?" said Richard trying desperately to give himself more time.

He had done nothing wrong. He tried to get his thoughts together while going into his contact list and dialled Anna's number.

"Hello handsome, it's good to...." Anna started.

"What did you do? Did you take the money? You thought I wouldn't find out?"

"What are you talking about?" Anna snapped back.

"I asked you to check the drawer, you are the only one who knew. You took the money. I am screwed".

"The drawer? You're the one who asked me to check it. I did nothing with your drawer. I told you it was locked," said Anna. "What are you accusing me of?".

"You stole my money." He was screaming now.

"It's not gonna end well asshole. I'm not your stupid girlfriend. How dare you talk to me like that!"

"You did, you took it-"

She had already hung up the phone. She decided to block his number immediately. He tried several times in desperation.

He couldn't believe it. How was this happening to him? He did not have the money. He was breathing heavily staring at his phone.

Kate. Kate had always been good to him, she would lend him the money. She had always vouched for him.

He called her but went straight to the voice mail again: "Hey babe, I need you. I have left you many messages. I know we have more to offer to each other. I realised how much I need you. Please give me a call."

Chapter 10

Kate woke up the next morning feeling numb from the day before. She went to the kitchen and turned the coffee machine on. She sipped and smelled the aroma as the sun was warming up the room. She was staying with Jack until she found a new flat to rent.

Sitting at the table, she checked her phone and started reading her emails.

She then opened the News app. Nothing interesting there either. Politics, she scrolled down, economics, interest rates were going up. She scrolled down and stopped at a small article from the local section.

Home invasion in Caulfield last night.

A man has been attacked in what seems to be a home invasion yesterday evening. The attackers have ransacked the house and the man was left injured. He is not in danger and has been admitted into hospital for observation.

Kate recognised the house in the photo. She knew who the man was. She had deleted every message and voice mail yesterday so she had no idea what happened. She wondered if she was responsible for that. But for once she did not torture herself.

Her first reaction was to check on him. She went into her contact list and paused, her finger hovering above his name. She closed her eyes and deleted the profile.

***

Two weeks later, Jack was preparing to leave for the Mornington Peninsula, when Kate called him from the kitchen.

"Look at that." Kate was on Facebook marketplace, looking for some furniture for her place.

"A tiger statue?" questioned Jack.

"Yes, I'm going to buy it", she said with a cheeky smile.

Jack was not sure what she meant, when suddenly he understood.

"No way is this?"

"Yes, I found out that Richard was selling some of his stuff. He needs money apparently."

"He wants $400 for the statue." In the throat of the tiger, there was a tiny opening. She was convinced the money she had hidden was still in there.

"I'll ask a friend to put in an offer", said Kate with a big smile.

"If Richard accepts, do you want to go somewhere fancy for dinner? What about 'Vue du Monde? Richard is paying."

RED ARC, BY REID FRANCIS
CHAPTER – WINDSOR, VIC

I moved when I got accepted into post-grad. My parents didn't understand why I'd want to study art. They'd worked hard to make sure I'd get to Uni, and they wanted me to be a lawyer. They let me do Fine Art in under-grad because I did it conjoint with Law, and they assumed the Art was just for fun. They figured if I became a lawyer, I'd never have to struggle like they did. And Law was fine, but painting was my passion and I was too good to give it up for a boring office job.

I'd never lived away from home before and I left all my friends and family behind to go to a new Uni in a different city. I found a single bedroom apartment with enough living space to set up my canvases and close to a train station on a line that'd get me straight to Uni. But my savings wouldn't cover rent, so getting a job was my first priority.

When I'd moved my stuff in, I went downstairs for a smoke – the thing with these flammable buildings is the balconies are useless if you need to get your nicotine fix. While I was down there, I noticed a bar just down the street a bit that looked interesting, so I wandered down to check it out. In a stroke of fantastic luck, there was a 'staff wanted' sign out front. That would be perfect – I'd worked in bars before, and mixing cocktails was an art-form I was almost as accomplished in as painting. It seemed to be a sign; this was obviously going to be a year to remember.

***

It's a weird feeling being rich and alone. When I was growing up, I could brush off the bullying and handle my loneliness because I knew I was going to be successful. My family was richer than anyone else I knew and I was smarter than most people I knew, so of course I was going to go further than them. I knew that they'd all want a piece of me then.

It all went according to plan – I started an IT business and made a fortune. Well, all except the popularity bit. Here I was in my late 30s with more money than I knew what to do with, but very few friends and somehow still single.

I comforted myself by spending my spare time at the bar down the road. The staff were friendly, the fried chicken was delicious and the drinks went down a treat. It made me feel at least a little bit connected to something and like I was actually welcome somewhere.

One night I walked in and there was a new girl behind the bar. She was stunning, but looked a little shier than most of the staff and the way she was dressed suggested she might've been a bit hard up – her clothes had holes in them, not in a stylised way, and there seemed to be flecks of paint all over them. Even at a dive bar that was unusual. I was intrigued.

Then I tasted her old fashioned and I knew I was in love! It takes someone special (and maybe someone putting an extra something special into it) to take a classic cocktail and produce something that blows your mind.

As I left that night, I dropped a couple of hundreds into the tip jar and let her know I'd be seeing her again.

***

The first night I saw him, something felt off. The way he stared. The way he winked when he dropped his tip into the jar. Maybe just his general vibe. But he tipped well and we all need the extra money. He's just a lonely awkward guy, I told myself, he's probably harmless.

From that night on, if I wasn't serving him, I always feel his eyes lingering on me. And those nights he didn't tip, he seemed to make quite a point of it in fact. So I tried to take one for the team and serve him whenever he came in. Those nights I need to take extra-long showers after work, I just felt so gross.

Thankfully it was only a few nights a week. The rest of the time I could throw myself into Uni – spending time in classes, painting in the studio, researching in the library, painting more when I got home. It was my happy place, and if I had to serve some creepy loner every now and then to make it happen then so be it.

But then one night I'd popped downstairs for a smoke break during a painting session and felt like someone was watching me. I looked across the street and there he was. Just standing and staring at me.

***

It got to the point where it wasn't enough to just see her at the bar. I was thinking about her constantly. And I was trying to find a way to make her mine.

But as if the gods were telling me it was meant to be, I got extraordinarily lucky. I was working from home one morning, in the front room on the ground floor of my apartment, and I looked up just as she walked by. There's no reason she'd be at the bar at that time – it didn't open again for hours – so that must mean she lived nearby!

I started working from home more and more. I would see what time she left, and what time she'd come home in the evening. I got to know her schedule pretty well, and I'd always be waiting at the window for her to come past. Even better, I could see the front door of her building from my window.

I stayed in my home office late some nights, eventually most nights, and hope she'd come out for a cigarette. One night it wasn't enough anymore to watch her through the window. I figured I needed to take my chance. So I slipped through the door, out onto the street, and stood watching her for a while, waiting for my opportunity to approach her. She must've felt the attraction too, because she looked right at me.

This was my moment! I started to cross the street towards her, but she threw away her half-smoked cigarette and rushed back inside.

***

Now it was genuinely starting to freak me out. He must know where I live. I needed to mix up my schedule. I'd take different trains. If I left Uni late, I'd catch an Uber. I cut back on smoking when I was home so he couldn't catch me on the street again. I started going to parties with my classmates; we weren't really friends but I figured I'd at least I'd be away from him and surrounded by other people.

I wasn't sleeping, my paintings were getting darker, and I just missed having my friends and family around me. Instead, I was here by myself trying to avoid this fucking creep.

Of course, I couldn't avoid him at work. I let my workmates know he was creeping me the fuck out and they tried to keep me away from him. The bouncers even started escorting me home after my shifts. But that didn't stop the staring. Or him trying to buy me drinks. Or getting annoyed when I turned down the offered drinks.

Then one weekend after finishing the day shift, I was sitting enjoying my burger with a whisky, and suddenly I felt someone looming over me. Of course it was him. He tried to sit down. 'That seat is taken', I told him. 'Doesn't look very taken to me, and I promise I'll make it worth your while', he replied. 'Seriously! Leave me the fuck alone!' I could feel my voice getting louder and louder.

Thankfully my workmate behind the bar saw what was happening and signalled the bouncer who kicked him out. I made sure he was barred.

**

I couldn't believe that bitch wouldn't even talk to me! And I couldn't even go back to my bar anymore. It was so fucking unfair!

Clearly, she didn't know what I could, what I would, give her. She'd have her own car, her own apartment, she'd never have to work again. Why wouldn't she give me the chance to show her what I can offer her?

I set up cameras on the street, so I could keep an eye on when she was coming and going. I spent every waking hour in my home office looking for the right opportunity. Her schedule was all over the place, but I had to find the right time to talk to her. I knew she'd say yes if she just heard me out. I'd have to force her to listen.

One morning I saw her on my cameras leaving home. I knew she must be heading to the train station, so I slipped through the front door, locked it and quickly headed to the station.

I got to the platform just as the train was arriving, so I jumped on and tried to squeeze my way past the morning commuters down the train to find her. As I neared the middle carriage, I saw her up ahead. It was the busiest carriage so I had to really shove my through.

Some douchebag gave me a shove back, which attracted attention. She saw me, then straightaway turned and fled, pushing past people and heading into the next carriage as we approached the next station.

I'd followed her before and she needed to get off in three stops, so I was certain she'd stay on. But for some reason, I couldn't make my way through people as quickly as she'd managed to and I lost sight of her. As we pulled out of the station, I looked outside saw her standing on the platform.

Dammit! I tried switching at the next station and heading back but when I got there, she was gone. I figured I'd have to try a different approach, one that'd be harder for her to get away from.

***

I was starting to get really worried for my life. Every now and then I'd notice the creep following me. The other day I even noticed him on the same train as me. Thankfully, it was busy enough that I managed to slip through the crowd and get away.

I was now severely limiting where I went – home, Uni, work, repeat. I mostly felt safe when I was there. I stopped smoking so I wouldn't be on the street alone. The bouncers protected me between work and home. But I knew travelling between home and Uni was where I was vulnerable. I couldn't afford to take an Uber every time though, so I had to try my luck with the train. Thankfully it was only 5 or 10 minutes to get to the station, and I was always hypervigilant. I started walking with my keys laced through my knuckles just in case. I even started to file the end of one key so it came to more of a point. I thought about calling the cops, but I didn't trust that they'd actually do anything.

I saw him watching me a lot, but at least he hadn't approached again. At least not yet,

My Uni work was suffering. I no longer had any motivation to paint, I didn't have the energy to do other assignments, readings or research. And I never called home anymore. I couldn't hide how I was feeling from my parents, but I couldn't tell them the truth because they'd just remind me that this wouldn't have happened if I'd stayed home and become a lawyer. As if that profession has a good history of treating women well.

Then one day I was walking home from the station and I saw him start walking towards me.

I gripped the keys tighter in my right fist. My hand started to throb.

'I just want to talk to you', he called as he approached.

'I told you to leave me alone!' I screamed.

'I've got an offer for you', he said, grabbing my left wrist, 'just hear me out'.

'There's nothing you could offer that I'd want!' I yelled, swinging my right fist at him.

I felt the key go into his neck. I saw the surprise in his eyes.

I felt relief as I pulled back, pulling the key out of his neck.

I watched as blood spurted out of his neck and over his pristine suit.

He crumpled onto the ground as life left his eyes.

I turned and ran home. Not out of fear though. I just had to get to my canvas. The huge arc blood, spurting from him, was one of the most beautiful, and liberating, things I'd ever seen.

I had to paint it.

TO SEE THE ALPS FOR THE PRICE OF A COBRA,
BY DECLAN MELIA
CHAPTER – COBURG, VIC

1. The briefcase

The boat's kerosene motor made a guttural choke as soon as my foot hit the dock and The Canary started back the way that it had come. I stood at the end of a long, crowded pier in my tatty tan suit with my head plumed in exhaust. From The Canary's landing point at the end of the pier to the sand-coloured concrete of the town was a gauntlet of activity. Porters in singlets and thongs shouted, sweated, and loaded. It was at this moment that I first felt a thump in the briefcase. Could the movement of the boat have woken it up? I convinced myself that I had imagined it. Tentatively, so as not to disturb it further, I began the walk down the pier, holding the hot, leather handle of the briefcase steady by my waist. As self-conscious as a child in the school hall. It was half past eight in the morning, but the sun was relentless. My sweat crystallised in my suit along with the splashes of saltwater from the overcrowded boat journey. My luggage was strapped across my chest, and when I used my left hand to shield my eyes, its strap twisted my thin blazer across my body grotesquely. I longed for my uniform, but the instructions had specifically read "civilian, formal". As out of place as I must have looked, no one paid me any regard. The local people too caught up in the demands of whichever micro-economy their manic toil served. I walked slowly so as to keep the briefcase steady and to avoid slipping on the slick boards of the pier. The position of my luggage was doing unusual things to my centre of gravity. Between the walls of commotion at the pier's outer edges I saw my name. A young man in black pants and black t-shirt held a sign.

Blue marker on an exercise book folded in on itself, the M and S in my last name in the wrong order. He leant on a sort of buggy, a two-stroke hybrid of a motorcycle and a carriage. He continued to hold the sign despite looking dead at me. There was certainly no one else on the dock that could bear my name or my purpose. He nodded as I stepped off the pier and onto the gravel of the waterfront, his face perfectly neutral. It seemed as though he wanted to shake my hand, but he was actually indicating that he wanted the luggage. I peeled the shoulder strap upwards and ducked my head and he loaded the bag onto the buggy. A band of sweat a salty sash across my front. The relief of being unburdened gave way to the embarrassment of being served and I winced inwardly as he helped me up onto the back of the bench seat of the buggy. I put the briefcase upwards on my knees and crossed my arms over it as meek as a tourist. I suppose that's what I was, certainly how I must appear. He started the motorbike and we peeled out onto a narrow, busy street. A faded souvenir stand, a boarded-up chemist, and a shadowy café advertising ice-cream. This time unmistakably, the briefcase moved. It was definitely awake. A marketplace, a motorcycle repair shop and then out towards the town.

2. The Contacio, Room 9

When I opened the door of Room 9 my luggage was sitting pleasingly at the foot of the bed. I laid the briefcase very gently on the tightly fitted sheets, stripped my suit and stood under the cold shower for a full twenty minutes. As I dried myself, I realised I was nervous. As if the snake was watching me through the front of the briefcase. I had never seen it; the briefcase was given to me locked, but I imagined it as patterned with bright colours. On the mainland, when they had entrusted me with it, they explained that it was asleep without offering any elaboration. Well, it was awake now. I imagined it perfectly coiled in the middle of the briefcase's belly, it's eyes white and alert. The fan squeaked above me as I dressed in the same suit that I had worn this morning. No point befouling my evening suit now. I checked the clock on the wall against the watch in my pocket and was surprised that they were perfectly aligned at five minutes to midday. Already too hot in my stiff shirt, I lifted the briefcase carefully off the bed, checked my hair in the mirror and left the room. I crossed the steaming garden slowly and tentatively passed back into the lobby. My room at The Contacio had been arranged for the sole purpose of this meeting and its very nature made me apprehensive. The Contacio lobby was roughly circular and dominated by a brass indoor fountain, the gurgling of which harmonised with the constant squeaking of the ceiling fans. The sound was not unpleasant. I entered the lobby to find it empty save a young man curled elaborately on one of the lounging chairs around the fountain, perhaps asleep. The sound of the opening and closing of the door did not alert him to my presence. His shoulder was turned at an uncomfortable angle, his chin on his shoulder. Like someone trying to sleep on a long-haul flight. Not for the first time today, I was surprised at how informally he was dressed, I had expected something more military. I cleared my throat as I walked towards him and he turned his head and smiled but did not speak or stand up. I came to a stop in front of him, unsure of what to do or say. It hadn't occurred to me that I would have to be the first to speak. I started to form a question, but it was as if he read my mind. 'Yes, it's me.' I couldn't place his accent. He gestured to the briefcase, 'It's in there?' I nodded and he held out his hand expectedly. I hesitated, a shy tourist bartering in a foreign bazaar.

'But. I. First' I stammered. He fished in his pocket and bought out a folded piece of note paper and offered it for me to take. I looked again around the lobby, the same receptionist shuffled papers on the other side of the fountain. 'It's the address and the time' he said with a hint of exasperation at my caution. I took the notepaper and held out the briefcase at the same time. He took it, not bothering with any of the caution that I had been using. Without more, my informer stood up and cricked his neck. He was much taller than me. As he turned and walked towards the street exit with the briefcase dangling by his side, I felt a sense of disappointment, as if I had expected something more coded, more criminal. I had the urge to shout a challenge as he walked away. How did he know it was me? How did he know the snake was in the briefcase? But I stood there as I had stood at the end of the pier, blinking and overwhelmed. I unfolded the paper and looked at the writing "36, The Corso, 2100 hours" written in sophisticated cursive. Again, I felt vaguely disappointed. Again, what did I expect?

3. Travelling

I arrived ten minutes late. Having been too cautious to ask the hotel for directions I had found 36 The Corso myself. It had grown dark early and I slunk in my evening suit through narrow alleyways and slipped under the shadows of buildings. It all seemed for naught; there was nobody - not a soul - around. The door to number 36 was smart and heavy, set in a tall concrete building. I looked over my shoulder. Seeing no one, I knocked. My blood icy with adrenaline. The door was opened by a middle-aged man with short white hair. He was, to my great relief, in uniform. He was, after all, a military man like me. He smiled pleasantly and gestured for me to enter. 'You're the last to arrive' he said without disparagement. The room within was lamp lit, tastefully furnished. Stairs led to a first floor. 'We're upstairs' he told me and began climbing, I followed. On a landing above were three closed doors. He opened the door on the right and we both passed through. My apprehension was making my limbs numb. The room lacked the ornate furnishings of the bottom floor. Exposed, dusty, floorboards lit by a weak, bare bulb and the obligatory squeaking ceiling fan. There were four mismatched wooden chairs all facing a squat cabinet against the opposite wall. Two of the seats were already occupied. One by a middle-aged woman in black clothes that looked like what one might see in a faded sepia photo and the other by a tall youth with round spectacles and a short black beard. The woman smiled at me nervously her hands clasped in her lap. The youth stared ahead with an air of impatience. I had expected there to be others, but I hadn't counted on how self-conscious their presence would cause me to be. I made a movement with my mouth, but not a sound. I sat down on one of the chairs and all of us other than the host were facing the cabinet. The player, with its baroque nobs and buttons was atop the cabinet, the entirety of which was actually a speaker. The youth crossed his arms and entwined his legs amongst the legs of the chair like straps of liquorice. Hunched over to take up as little space in the room as possible. His fingernails were long and dirty. Our host, who in the context of the bare room appeared needlessly fastidious in his uniform, leaned on the cabinet and turned a nob on the player which made a muffled sound. 'Since we're all here, we'll get started' he said and reached behind the cabinet. My nerves intensified. Would my fellow travellers be able to discern that it was my first time? What if I broke into ecstatic seizure? If I'm in a state of seizure perhaps I won't care so much what strangers think of me, I reasoned unconvincingly to myself. Our host returned from his rummage behind the speaker and held the square of the record cover in front of his chest. A picture of a Swiss looking hillside with a mountain in the background. In far better condition than one might have imagined. I didn't recognise the name. I had heard of Beethoven and Bach, but that was all. The title proclaimed that the music was in the key of C. My mind was racing. How many did he have back there? How had he procured them? Whose safety had been compromised so that the four of us might meet here, on the other side of the earth, to enjoy this most decadent and criminal of moments? The dinner with the Colonel, the boat ride, the snake in the briefcase, the pier and the hotel. I take it all back, I'm not ready! Good god! He was drawing the black disc out of the cover. The apprehension in the room was suffocating. I tried my best to stifle my breath and leaned forward in the seat. 'Is everyone ready?' he asked. The woman made a gentle humming noise and the youth and I nodded at the same time. He slid the record onto the platter and the needle hit the disk with a noise like a breath heard from within the body. Suddenly it was upon us. Good God. A conduction like the sigh of angels. A feeling not unlike falling asleep while satisfyingly drunk or awaking from a summer nap. I closed my eyes – or they closed by themselves - and I saw images of a Swiss hillside and tall blue mountains.

Thanks
This book would not have been made without the hard work
and dedication of our club members.

Each person involved donated their time and energy to help us
get this book published. We would like to give our thanks to the
following Goons:
Daniel Carlin, Chris Capetanakis, Dave Cheetham, John Dalton,
Chas Lang, Brent Lowrey, Peter Machell, Guy Metcalfe,
David Michell, Darren Saffin, Brad Snoey, and Andrew Thomas.

Other books read by the Tough Guy Book Club

Metamorphosis – Franz Kafka (1913)

The Outsiders – S.E. Hinton (1967)

The Magician – Colm Tóibín (2021)

Wolf In White Van – John Darnielle (2014)

The Glass Canoe – David Ireland (1976)

The Great Gatsby – F. Scott Fitzgerald (1925)*

400 Days – Chetan Bhagat (2021)

One Flew Over The Cuckoo's Nest – Ken Kesey (1962)

Sharks In The Time Of Saviours – Kawai Strong Washburn (2020)

The Gun – C.S. Forester (1933)*

All Systems Red – Martha Wells (2017)

The Road – Cormac McCarthy (2006)

Farewell, My Lovely – Raymond Chandler (1940)

The Amazing Adventures Of Kavalier & Clay – Michael Chabon (2000)

The Age Of Reason – Jean-Paul Sartre (1945)

Last Orders – Graham Swift (1996)

Station Eleven – Emily St. John Mandel (2014)

Breakfast Of Champions – Kurt Vonnegut (1973)

The Snows Of Kilimanjaro – Ernest Hemingway (1936)

The Talented Mr. Ripley – Patricia Highsmith (1955)

The Master And Margarita – Mikhail Bulgakov (1973)

The Hawkline Monster – Richard Brautigan (1974)

Notes From Underground – Fyodor Dostoevsky (1864)

Breath – Tim Winton (2008)

The Starless Sea – Erin Morgenstern (2019)

Frankenstein In Baghdad – Ahmed Saadawi (2013)

Fahrenheit 451 – Ray Bradbury (1953)

White Teeth – Zadie Smith (2000)

High Fidelity – Nick Hornby (1995)

The Water Dancer – Ta-Nehisi Coates (2019)

Cannery Row – John Steinbeck (1945)

The Martian – Andy Weir (2011)

The Messenger – Markus Zusak (2002)

A Man Called Ove – Fredrik Backman (2012)

Last Exit To Brooklyn – Hubert Selby Jr (1964)

Hornblower And The Hotspur – C. S. Forester (1962)

Trainspotting – Irvine Welsh (1993)

To Name Those Lost – Rohan Wilson (2014)

Hell's Angels – Hunter S. Thompson (1967)

Drive Your Plow Over The Bones Of The Dead – Olga Tokarczuk (2009)

A Visit From The Goon Squad – Jennifer Egan (2010)

For Whom The Bell Tolls – Ernest Hemingway (1940)

Praise – Andrew McGahan (1995)

Go Tell It On The Mountain – James Baldwin (1953)

Small Gods – Terry Pratchett (1992)

Stoner – John Williams (1965)

Ask The Dust – John Fante (1939)

Neuromancer – William Gibson (1984)

The Things They Carried – Tim O'Brien (1990)

Men Without Women – Haruki Murakami (2014)

The Plains – Gerald Murnane (1982)

The Spy Who Came In From The Cold – John Le Carré (1963)

Things Fall Apart – Chinua Achebe (1959)

Men Without Women – Ernest Hemingway (1927)

The Eye Of The Sheep – Sofie Laguna (2014)

The Hitchhiker's Guide To The Galaxy – Douglas Adams (1979)

That Deadman Dance – Kim Scott (2010)

As I Lay Dying – William Faulkner (1930)

The Adventures Of Sherlock Holmes – Arthur Conan Doyle (1892)

East Of Eden – John Steinbeck (1952)

Johnno – David Malouf (1975)

Ham On Rye – Charles Bukowski (1982)

Death Of A River Guide – Richard Flanagan (1994)

God Bless You, Mr. Rosewater – Kurt Vonnegut (1965)

The Dispossessed – Ursula K. Le Guin (1974)

The Old Man And The Sea – Ernest Hemingway (1952)

The Big Nowhere – James Ellroy (1988)

Home – Toni Morrison (2012)

The Jesus Man – Christos Tsiolkas (1999)

Good Omens – Pratchett & Gaiman (1990)

On The Road – Jack Kerouac (1957)

A Brief History Of Seven Killings – Marlon James (2015)

Blood Meridian – Cormac McCarthy (1985)

Brave New World – Aldous Huxley (1932)

The Roving Party – Rohan Wilson (2011)

Trout Fishing In America – Richard Brautigan (1967)

Casino Royal – Ian Fleming (1953)

A Farewell To Arms – Ernest Hemmingway (1929)

Death In Brunswick – Boyd Oxlade (1987)

To Kill A Mockingbird – Harper Lee (1960)

Rumble Fish – S. E. Hinton (1975)

Wake In Fright – Kenneth Cook (1961)

Our Man In Havana – Graham Greene (1958)

American Gods – Neil Gaiman (2001)

The Big Sleep – Raymond Chandler (1939)

The Sisters Brothers – Patrick Dewitt (2011)

The Sound Of Things Falling – Juan Gabriel Vásquez (2011)

The Sun Also Rises – Ernest Hemingway (1962)

I Am Pilgrim – Terry Hayes (2013)

Rabbit, Run – John Updike (1960)

A Clockwork Orange – Anthony Burgess (1962)

Brighton Rock – Graham Greene (1938)

Post Office – Charles Bukowski (1971)

Catch–22 – Joseph Heller (1961)

The Martian – Andy Weir (2012)

The Rum Diary – Hunter S. Thompson (1998)

The Fight – Norman Mailer (1975)

The Razor's Edge – W. Somerset Maugham (1944)

The Call Of The Wild – Jack London (1903)

Heart Of Darkness – Joseph Conrad (1899)

Machine Man – Max Barry (2006)

*A Tough Guy Book Club publication